THE ETERNAL MOMENT, AND OTHER STORIES

By E. M. Forster

NATAL PUBLISHING LLC
ARS LONGA, VITA BREVIS

Copyright© 2024 Natal Publishing

THE MACHINE STOPS

Part I
THE AIR-SHIP

Imagine, if you can, a small room, hexagonal in shape, like the cell of a bee. It is lighted neither by window nor by lamp, yet it is filled with a soft radiance. There are no apertures for ventilation, yet the air is fresh. There are no musical instruments, and yet, at the moment that my meditation opens, this room is throbbing with melodious sounds. An arm-chair is in the centre, by its side a reading-desk—that is all the furniture. And in the arm-chair there sits a swaddled lump of flesh—a woman, about five feet high, with a face as white as a fungus. It is to her that the little room belongs.

An electric bell rang.

The woman touched a switch and the music was silent.

"I suppose I must see who it is," she thought, and set her chair in motion. The chair, like the music, was worked by machinery, and it rolled her to the other side of the room, where the bell still rang importunately.

"Who is it?" she called. Her voice was irritable, for she had been interrupted often since the music began. She knew several thousand people; in certain directions human intercourse had advanced enormously.

But when she listened into the receiver, her white face wrinkled into smiles, and she said:

"Very well. Let us talk, I will isolate myself. I do not expect anything important will happen for the next five minutes—for I can give you fully five minutes, Kuno. Then I must deliver my lecture on 'Music during the Australian Period.'"

She touched the isolation knob, so that no one else could speak to her. Then she touched the lighting apparatus, and the little room was plunged into darkness.

"Be quick!" she called, her irritation returning. "Be quick, Kuno; here I am in the dark wasting my time."

But it was fully fifteen seconds before the round plate that she held in her hands began to glow. A faint blue light shot across it, darkening to purple, and presently she could see the image of her son, who lived on the other side of the earth, and he could see her.

"Kuno, how slow you are."

He smiled gravely.

"I really believe you enjoy dawdling."

"I have called you before, mother, but you were always busy or isolated. I have something particular to say."

"What is it, dearest boy? Be quick. Why could you not send it by pneumatic post?"

"Because I prefer saying such a thing. I want——"

"Well?"

"I want you to come and see me."

Vashti watched his face in the blue plate.

"But I can see you!" she exclaimed. "What more do you want?"

"I want to see you not through the Machine," said Kuno. "I want to speak to you not through the wearisome Machine."

"Oh, hush!" said his mother, vaguely shocked. "You mustn't say anything against the Machine."

"Why not?"

"One mustn't."

"You talk as if a god had made the Machine," cried the other. "I believe that you pray to it when you are unhappy. Men made it, do not forget that. Great men, but men. The Machine is much, but it is not everything. I see something like you in this plate, but I do not see you. I hear something like you through this telephone, but I do not hear you. That is why I want you to come. Come and stop with me. Pay me a visit, so that we can meet face to face, and talk about the hopes that are in my mind."

She replied that she could scarcely spare the time for a visit.

"The air-ship barely takes two days to fly between me and you."

"I dislike air-ships."

"Why?"

"I dislike seeing the horrible brown earth, and the sea, and the stars when it is dark. I get no ideas in an air-ship."

"I do not get them anywhere else."

"What kind of ideas can the air give you?"

He paused for an instant.

"Do you not know four big stars that form an oblong, and three stars close together in the middle of the oblong, and hanging from these stars, three other stars?"

"No, I do not. I dislike the stars. But did they give you an idea? How interesting; tell me."

"I had an idea that they were like a man."

"I do not understand."

"The four big stars are the man's shoulders and his knees. The three stars in the middle are like the belts that men wore once, and the three stars hanging are like a sword."

"A sword?"

"Men carried swords about with them, to kill animals and other men."

"It does not strike me as a very good idea, but it is certainly original. When did it come to you first?"

"In the air-ship——" He broke off, and she fancied that he looked sad. She could not be sure, for the Machine did not transmit *nuances* of expression. It only gave a general idea of people—an idea that was good enough for all practical purposes, Vashti thought. The imponderable bloom, declared by a discredited philosophy to be the actual essence of intercourse, was rightly ignored by the Machine, just as the imponderable bloom of the grape was ignored by the manufacturers of artificial fruit. Something "good enough" had long since been accepted by our race.

"The truth is," he continued, "that I want to see these stars again. They are curious stars. I want to see them not from the air-ship, but from the surface of the earth, as our ancestors did, thousands of years ago. I want to visit the surface of the earth."

She was shocked again.

"Mother, you must come, if only to explain to me what is the harm of visiting the surface of the earth."

"No harm," she replied, controlling herself. "But no advantage. The surface of the earth is only dust and mud, no life remains on it, and you would need a respirator, or the cold of the outer air would kill you. One dies immediately in the outer air."

"I know; of course I shall take all precautions."

"And besides——"

"Well?"

She considered, and chose her words with care. Her son had a queer temper, and she wished to dissuade him from the expedition.

"It is contrary to the spirit of the age," she asserted.

"Do you mean by that, contrary to the Machine?"

"In a sense, but——"

His image in the blue plate faded.

"Kuno!"

He had isolated himself.

For a moment Vashti felt lonely.

Then she generated the light, and the sight of her room, flooded with radiance and studded with electric buttons, revived her. There were buttons and switches everywhere—buttons to call for food, for music, for clothing. There was the hot-bath button, by pressure of which a basin of (imitation) marble rose out of the floor, filled to the brim with a warm deodorised liquid. There was the cold-bath button. There was the button that produced literature. And there were of course the buttons by which she communicated with her friends. The room, though it contained nothing, was in touch with all that she cared for in the world.

Vashti's next move was to turn off the isolation-switch, and all the accumulations of the last three minutes burst upon her. The room was filled with the noise of bells, and speaking-tubes. What was the new food like? Could she recommend it? Had she had any ideas lately? Might one tell her one's own ideas? Would she make an engagement to visit the public nurseries at an early date?—say this day month.

To most of these questions she replied with irritation—a growing quality in that accelerated age. She said that the new food was horrible. That she could not visit the public nurseries through press of engagements. That she had no ideas of her own but had just been told one—that four stars and three in the middle were like a man: she doubted there was much in it. Then she switched off her correspondents, for it was time to deliver her lecture on Australian music.

The clumsy system of public gatherings had been long since abandoned; neither Vashti nor her audience stirred from their rooms. Seated in her arm-chair she spoke, while they in their arm-chairs heard her, fairly well, and saw her, fairly well. She opened with a humorous account of music in the pre-Mongolian epoch, and went on to describe the great outburst of song that followed the Chinese conquest. Remote and primæval as were the methods of I-San-So and the Brisbane school, she yet felt (she said) that study of them might repay the musician of today: they had freshness; they had, above all, ideas.

Her lecture, which lasted ten minutes, was well received, and at its conclusion she and many of her audience listened to a lecture on the sea; there were ideas to be got from the sea; the speaker had donned a respirator and visited it lately. Then she fed, talked to many friends, had a bath, talked again, and summoned her bed.

The bed was not to her liking. It was too large, and she had a feeling for a small bed. Complaint was useless, for beds were of the same dimension all over the world, and to have had an alternative size would have involved vast alterations in the Machine. Vashti isolated herself—it was necessary, for neither day nor night existed under the ground—and reviewed all that had happened since she had summoned the bed last. Ideas? Scarcely any. Events—was Kuno's invitation an event?

By her side, on the little reading-desk, was a survival from the ages of litter—one book. This was the Book of the Machine. In it were instructions against every possible contingency. If she was hot or cold or dyspeptic or at loss for a word, she went to the book, and it told her which button to press. The Central Committee published it. In accordance with a growing habit, it was richly bound.

Sitting up in the bed, she took it reverently in her hands. She glanced round the glowing room as if some one might be watching her. Then, half ashamed, half joyful, she murmured "O Machine! O Machine!" and raised the volume to her lips. Thrice she kissed it, thrice inclined her head, thrice she felt the delirium of acquiescence. Her ritual performed, she turned to page 1367, which gave the times of the departure of the air-ships from the island in the southern hemisphere, under whose soil she lived, to the island in the northern hemisphere, whereunder lived her son.

She thought, "I have not the time."

She made the room dark and slept; she awoke and made the room light; she ate and exchanged ideas with her friends, and listened to music and attended lectures; she made the room dark and slept. Above her, beneath her, and around her, the Machine hummed eternally; she did not notice the noise, for she had been born with it in her ears. The earth, carrying her, hummed as it sped through silence, turning her now to the invisible sun, now to the invisible stars. She awoke and made the room light.

"Kuno!"

"I will not talk to you," he answered, "until you come."

"Have you been on the surface of the earth since we spoke last?"

His image faded.

Again she consulted the book. She became very nervous and lay back in her chair palpitating. Think of her as without teeth or hair. Presently she directed the chair to the wall, and pressed an unfamiliar button. The wall swung apart slowly. Through the opening she saw a tunnel that curved slightly, so that its goal was not visible. Should she go to see her son, here was the beginning of the journey.

Of course she knew all about the communication-system. There was nothing mysterious in it. She would summon a car and it would fly with her down the tunnel until it reached the lift that communicated with the air-ship station: the system had been in use for many, many years, long before the universal establishment of the Machine. And of course she had studied the civilisation that had immediately preceded her own—the civilisation that had mistaken the functions of the system, and had used it for bringing people to things, instead of for bringing things to people. Those funny old days, when men went for change of air instead of changing the air in their rooms! And yet—she was frightened of the tunnel: she had not seen it since her last child was born. It curved—but not quite as she remembered; it was brilliant—but not quite as brilliant as a lecturer had suggested. Vashti was seized with the terrors of direct experience. She shrank back into the room, and the wall closed up again.

"Kuno," she said, "I cannot come to see you. I am not well."

Immediately an enormous apparatus fell on to her out of the ceiling, a thermometer was automatically inserted between her lips, a stethoscope was automatically laid upon her heart. She lay powerless. Cool pads soothed her forehead. Kuno had telegraphed to her doctor.

So the human passions still blundered up and down in the Machine. Vashti drank the medicine that the doctor projected into her mouth, and the machinery retired into the ceiling. The voice of Kuno was heard asking how she felt.

"Better." Then with irritation: "But why do you not come to me instead?"

"Because I cannot leave this place."

"Why?"

"Because, any moment, something tremendous may happen."

"Have you been on the surface of the earth yet?"

"Not yet."

"Then what is it?"

"I will not tell you through the Machine."

She resumed her life.

But she thought of Kuno as a baby, his birth, his removal to the public nurseries, her one visit to him there, his visits to her—visits which stopped when the Machine had assigned him a room on the other side of the earth. "Parents, duties of," said the book of the Machine, "cease at the moment of birth. P. 422327483." True, but there was something special about Kuno—indeed there had been something special about all her children—and, after all, she must brave the journey if he desired it. And "something tremendous might happen." What did that mean? The nonsense of a youthful man, no doubt, but she must go. Again she pressed the unfamiliar button, again the wall swung back, and she saw the tunnel that curved out of sight. Clasping the Book, she rose, tottered on to the platform, and summoned the car. Her room closed behind her: the journey to the northern hemisphere had begun.

Of course it was perfectly easy. The car approached and in it she found arm-chairs exactly like her own. When she signalled, it stopped, and she tottered into the lift. One other passenger was in the lift, the first fellow creature she had seen face to face for months. Few travelled in these days, for, thanks to the advance of science, the earth was exactly alike all over. Rapid intercourse, from which the previous civilisation had hoped so much, had ended by defeating itself. What was the good of going to Pekin when it was just like Shrewsbury? Why return to Shrewsbury when it would be just like Pekin? Men seldom moved their bodies; all unrest was concentrated in the soul.

The air-ship service was a relic from the former age. It was kept up, because it was easier to keep it up than to stop it or to diminish it, but it now far exceeded the wants of the population. Vessel after vessel would rise from the vomitories of Rye or of Christchurch (I use the antique names), would sail into the crowded sky, and would draw up at the wharves of the south—empty. So nicely adjusted was the system, so independent of meteorology, that the sky, whether calm or cloudy, resembled a vast kaleidoscope whereon the same patterns periodically recurred. The ship on which Vashti sailed started now at sunset, now at dawn. But always, as it passed above Rheims, it would neighbour the ship that served between Helsingfors and the Brazils, and, every third time it surmounted the Alps, the fleet of Palermo would cross its track behind. Night and day, wind and storm, tide and earthquake, impeded man no longer. He had harnessed Leviathan. All the old literature, with its praise of Nature, and its fear of Nature, rang false as the prattle of a child.

Yet as Vashti saw the vast flank of the ship, stained with exposure to the outer air, her horror of direct experience returned. It was not quite like the air-ship in the cinematophote. For one thing it smelt—not strongly or unpleasantly, but it did smell, and with her eyes shut she should have known that a new thing was close to her. Then she had to walk to it from the lift, had to submit to glances from the other passengers. The man in front dropped his Book—no great matter, but it disquieted them all. In the rooms, if the Book was dropped, the floor raised it mechanically, but the gangway to the air-ship was not so prepared, and the sacred volume lay motionless. They stopped—the thing was unforeseen—and the man, instead of picking up his property, felt the muscles of his arm to see how they had failed him. Then some one actually said with direct utterance: "We shall be late"—and they trooped on board, Vashti treading on the pages as she did so.

Inside, her anxiety increased. The arrangements were old-fashioned and rough. There was even a female attendant, to whom she would have to announce her wants during the voyage. Of course a revolving platform ran the length of the boat, but she was expected to walk from it to her cabin. Some cabins were better than others, and she did not get the best. She thought the attendant had been unfair, and spasms of rage shook her. The glass valves had closed, she could not go back. She saw, at the end of the vestibule, the lift in which she had ascended going quietly up and down, empty. Beneath those corridors of shining tiles were rooms, tier below tier, reaching far into the earth, and in each room there sat a human being, eating, or sleeping, or producing ideas. And buried deep in the hive was her own room. Vashti was afraid.

"O Machine! O Machine!" she murmured, and caressed her Book, and was comforted.

Then the sides of the vestibule seemed to melt together, as do the passages that we see in dreams, the lift vanished, the Book that had been dropped slid to the left and vanished, polished tiles rushed by like a stream of water, there was a slight jar, and the air-ship, issuing from its tunnel, soared above the waters of a tropical ocean.

It was night. For a moment she saw the coast of Sumatra edged by the phosphorescence of waves, and crowned by lighthouses, still sending forth their disregarded beams. These also vanished, and only the stars distracted her. They were not motionless, but swayed to and fro above her head, thronging out of one skylight into another, as if the universe and not the air-ship was careening. And, as often happens on clear nights, they seemed now to be in perspective, now on a plane; now piled tier beyond tier into the infinite heavens, now concealing infinity, a roof limiting for ever the visions of men. In either case they seemed intolerable. "Are we to travel in the dark?" called the passengers angrily, and the attendant, who had been careless, generated the light, and pulled down the blinds of pliable metal. When the air-ships had been built, the desire to look direct at things still lingered in the world. Hence the extraordinary number of skylights and windows, and the proportionate discomfort to those who were civilised and refined. Even in Vashti's cabin one star peeped through a flaw in the blind, and after a few hours' uneasy slumber, she was disturbed by an unfamiliar glow, which was the dawn.

Quick as the ship had sped westwards, the earth had rolled eastwards quicker still, and had dragged back Vashti and her companions towards the sun. Science could prolong the night, but only for a little, and those high hopes of neutralising the earth's diurnal revolution had passed, together with hopes that were possibly higher. To "keep pace with the sun," or even to outstrip it, had been the aim of the civilisation preceding this. Racing aeroplanes had been built for the purpose, capable of enormous speed, and steered by the greatest intellects of the epoch. Round the globe they went, round and round, westward, westward, round and round, amidst humanity's applause. In vain. The globe went eastward quicker still, horrible accidents occurred, and the Committee of the Machine, at the time rising into prominence, declared the pursuit illegal, unmechanical, and punishable by Homelessness.

Of Homelessness more will be said later.

Doubtless the Committee was right. Yet the attempt to "defeat the sun" aroused the last common interest that our race experienced about the heavenly bodies, or indeed about anything. It was the last time that men were compacted by thinking of a power outside the world. The sun had conquered, yet it was the end of his spiritual dominion. Dawn, midday, twilight, the zodiacal path, touched neither men's lives nor their hearts, and science retreated into the ground, to concentrate herself upon problems that she was certain of solving.

So when Vashti found her cabin invaded by a rosy finger of light, she was annoyed, and tried to adjust the blind. But the blind flew up altogether, and she saw through the skylight small pink clouds, swaying against a background of blue, and as the sun crept higher, its radiance entered direct, brimming down the wall, like a golden sea. It rose and fell with the air-ship's motion, just as waves rise and fall, but it advanced steadily, as a tide advances. Unless she was careful, it would strike her face. A spasm of horror shook her and she rang for the attendant. The attendant too was horrified, but she could do nothing; it was not her place to mend the blind. She could only suggest that the lady should change her cabin, which she accordingly prepared to do.

People were almost exactly alike all over the world, but the attendant of the air-ship, perhaps owing to her exceptional duties, had grown a little out of the common. She had often to address passengers with direct speech, and this had given her a certain roughness and originality of manner. When

Vashti swerved away from the sunbeams with a cry, she behaved barbarically—she put out her hand to steady her.

"How dare you!" exclaimed the passenger. "You forget yourself!"

The woman was confused, and apologised for not having let her fall. People never touched one another. The custom had become obsolete, owing to the Machine.

"Where are we now?" asked Vashti haughtily.

"We are over Asia," said the attendant, anxious to be polite.

"Asia?"

"You must excuse my common way of speaking. I have got into the habit of calling places over which I pass by their unmechanical names."

"Oh, I remember Asia. The Mongols came from it."

"Beneath us, in the open air, stood a city that was once called Simla."

"Have you ever heard of the Mongols and of the Brisbane school?"

"No."

"Brisbane also stood in the open air."

"Those mountains to the right—let me show you them." She pushed back a metal blind. The main chain of the Himalayas was revealed. "They were once called the Roof of the World, those mountains."

"What a foolish name!"

"You must remember that, before the dawn of civilisation, they seemed to be an impenetrable wall that touched the stars. It was supposed that no one but the gods could exist above their summits. How we have advanced, thanks to the Machine!"

"How we have advanced, thanks to the Machine!" said Vashti.

"How we have advanced, thanks to the Machine!" echoed the passenger who had dropped his Book the night before, and who was standing in the passage.

"And that white stuff in the cracks?—what is it?"

"I have forgotten its name."

"Cover the window, please. These mountains give me no ideas."

The northern aspect of the Himalayas was in deep shadow: on the Indian slope the sun had just prevailed. The forests had been destroyed during the literature epoch for the purpose of making newspaper-pulp, but the snows were awakening to their morning glory, and clouds still hung on the breasts of Kinchinjunga. In the plain were seen the ruins of cities, with diminished rivers creeping by their walls, and by the sides of these were sometimes the signs of vomitories, marking the cities of today. Over the whole prospect air-ships rushed, crossing and intercrossing with incredible *aplomb*, and rising nonchalantly when they desired to escape the perturbations of the lower atmosphere and to traverse the Roof of the World.

"We have indeed advanced, thanks to the Machine," repeated the attendant, and hid the Himalayas behind a metal blind.

The day dragged wearily forward. The passengers sat each in his cabin, avoiding one another with an almost physical repulsion and longing to be once more under the surface of the earth. There were eight or ten of them, mostly young males, sent out from the public nurseries to inhabit the rooms of those who had died in various parts of the earth. The man who had dropped his Book was on the homeward journey. He had been sent to Sumatra for the purpose of propagating the race. Vashti alone was travelling by her private will.

At midday she took a second glance at the earth. The air-ship was crossing another range of mountains, but she could see little, owing to clouds. Masses of black rock hovered below her, and merged indistinctly into grey. Their shapes were fantastic; one of them resembled a prostrate man.

"No ideas here," murmured Vashti, and hid the Caucasus behind a metal blind.

In the evening she looked again. They were crossing a golden sea, in which lay many small islands and one peninsula.

She repeated, "No ideas here," and hid Greece behind a metal blind.

Part II
THE MENDING APPARATUS

By a vestibule, by a lift, by a tubular railway, by a platform, by a sliding door—by reversing all the steps of her departure did Vashti arrive at her son's room, which exactly resembled her own. She might well declare that the visit was superfluous. The buttons, the knobs, the reading-desk with the Book, the temperature, the atmosphere, the illumination—all were exactly the same. And if Kuno himself, flesh of her flesh, stood close beside her at last, what profit was there in that? She was too well-bred to shake him by the hand.

Averting her eyes, she spoke as follows:

"Here I am. I have had the most terrible journey and greatly retarded the development of my soul. It is not worth it, Kuno, it is not worth it. My time is too precious. The sunlight almost touched me, and I have met with the rudest people. I can only stop a few minutes. Say what you want to say, and then I must return."

"I have been threatened with Homelessness," said Kuno.

She looked at him now.

"I have been threatened with Homelessness, and I could not tell you such a thing through the Machine."

Homelessness means death. The victim is exposed to the air, which kills him.

"I have been outside since I spoke to you last. The tremendous thing has happened, and they have discovered me."

"But why shouldn't you go outside!" she exclaimed. "It is perfectly legal, perfectly mechanical, to visit the surface of the earth. I have lately been to a lecture on the sea; there is no objection to that; one simply summons a respirator and gets an Egression-permit. It is not the kind of thing that spiritually-minded people do, and I begged you not to do it, but there is no legal objection to it."

"I did not get an Egression-permit."

"Then how did you get out?"

"I found out a way of my own."

The phrase conveyed no meaning to her, and he had to repeat it.

"A way of your own?" she whispered. "But that would be wrong."

"Why?"

The question shocked her beyond measure.

"You are beginning to worship the Machine," he said coldly. "You think it irreligious of me to have found out a way of my own. It was just what the Committee thought, when they threatened me with Homelessness."

At this she grew angry. "I worship nothing!" she cried. "I am most advanced. I don't think you irreligious, for there is no such thing as religion left. All the fear and the superstition that existed once have been destroyed by the Machine. I only meant that to find out a way of your own was—— Besides, there is no new way out."

"So it is always supposed."

"Except through the vomitories, for which one must have an Egression-permit, it is impossible to get out. The Book says so."

"Well, the Book's wrong, for I have been out on my feet."

For Kuno was possessed of a certain physical strength.

By these days it was a demerit to be muscular. Each infant was examined at birth, and all who promised undue strength were destroyed. Humanitarians may protest, but it would have been no true kindness to let an athlete live; he would never have been happy in that state of life to which the Machine had called him; he would have yearned for trees to climb, rivers to bathe in, meadows and hills against which he might measure his body. Man must be adapted to his surroundings, must he not? In the dawn of the world our weakly must be exposed on Mount Taygetus, in its twilight our strong will suffer euthanasia, that the Machine may progress, that the Machine may progress, that the Machine may progress eternally.

"You know that we have lost the sense of space. We say 'space is annihilated,' but we have annihilated not space, but the sense thereof. We have lost a part of ourselves. I determined to recover it, and I began by walking up and down the platform of the railway outside my room. Up and down, until I was tired, and so did recapture the meaning of 'Near' and 'Far.' 'Near' is a place to which I can get quickly *on my feet*, not a place to which the train or the air-ship will take me quickly. 'Far' is a place to which I cannot get quickly on my feet; the vomitory is 'far,' though I could be there in thirty-eight seconds by summoning the train. Man is the measure. That was my first lesson. Man's feet are the measure for distance, his hands are the measure for ownership, his body is the measure for all that is lovable and desirable and strong. Then I went further: it was then that I called to you for the first time, and you would not come.

"This city, as you know, is built deep beneath the surface of the earth, with only the vomitories protruding. Having paced the platform outside my own room, I took the lift to the next platform and paced that also, and so with each in turn, until I came to the topmost, above which begins the earth. All the platforms were exactly alike, and all that I gained by visiting them was to develop my sense of space and my muscles. I think I should have been content with this—it is not a little thing—but as I walked and brooded, it occurred to me that our cities had been built in the days when men still breathed the outer air, and that there had been ventilation shafts for the workmen. I could think of nothing but these ventilation shafts. Had they been destroyed by all the food-tubes and medicine-tubes and music-tubes that the Machine has evolved lately? Or did traces of them remain? One thing was certain. If I came upon them anywhere, it would be in the railway-tunnels of the topmost story. Everywhere else, all space was accounted for.

"I am telling my story quickly, but don't think that I was not a coward or that your answers never depressed me. It is not the proper thing, it is not mechanical, it is not decent to walk along a railway-tunnel. I did not fear that I might tread upon a live rail and be killed. I feared something far more intangible—doing what was not contemplated by the Machine. Then I said to myself, 'Man is the measure,' and I went, and after many visits I found an opening.

"The tunnels, of course, were lighted. Everything is light, artificial light; darkness is the exception. So when I saw a black gap in the tiles, I knew that it was an exception, and rejoiced. I put in my arm—I could put in no more at first—and waved it round and round in ecstasy. I loosened another tile, and put in my head, and shouted into the darkness: 'I am coming, I shall do it yet,' and my voice reverberated down endless passages. I seemed to hear the spirits of those dead workmen who had returned each evening to the starlight and to their wives, and all the generations who had lived in the open air called back to me, 'You will do it yet, you are coming.'"

He paused, and, absurd as he was, his last words moved her. For Kuno had lately asked to be a father, and his request had been refused by the Committee. His was not a type that the Machine desired to hand on.

"Then a train passed. It brushed by me, but I thrust my head and arms into the hole. I had done enough for one day, so I crawled back to the platform, went down in the lift, and summoned my bed. Ah, what dreams! And again I called you, and again you refused."

She shook her head and said:

"Don't. Don't talk of these terrible things. You make me miserable. You are throwing civilisation away."

"But I had got back the sense of space and a man cannot rest then. I determined to get in at the hole and climb the shaft. And so I exercised my arms. Day after day I went through ridiculous movements, until my flesh ached, and I could hang by my hands and hold the pillow of my bed outstretched for many minutes. Then I summoned a respirator, and started.

"It was easy at first. The mortar had somehow rotted, and I soon pushed some more tiles in, and clambered after them into the darkness, and the spirits of the dead comforted me. I don't know what I mean by that. I just say what I felt. I felt, for the first time, that a protest had been lodged against corruption, and that even as the dead were comforting me, so I was comforting the unborn. I felt that humanity existed, and that it existed without clothes. How can I possibly explain this? It was naked, humanity seemed naked, and all these tubes and buttons and machineries neither came into the world with us, nor will they follow us out, nor do they matter supremely while we are here. Had I been strong, I would have torn off every garment I had, and gone out into the outer air unswaddled. But this is not for me, nor perhaps for my generation. I climbed with my respirator and my hygienic clothes and my dietetic tabloids! Better thus than not at all.

"There was a ladder, made of some primæval metal. The light from the railway fell upon its lowest rungs, and I saw that it led straight upwards out of the rubble at the bottom of the shaft. Perhaps our ancestors ran up and down it a dozen times daily, in their building. As I climbed, the rough edges cut through my gloves so that my hands bled. The light helped me for a little, and then came darkness and, worse still, silence which pierced my ears like a sword. The Machine hums! Did you know that? Its hum penetrates our blood, and may even guide our thoughts. Who knows! I was getting beyond its power. Then I thought: 'This silence means that I am doing wrong.' But I heard voices in the silence, and again they strengthened me." He laughed. "I had need of them. The next moment I cracked my head against something."

She sighed.

"I had reached one of those pneumatic stoppers that defend us from the outer air. You may have noticed them on the air-ship. Pitch dark, my feet on the rungs of an invisible ladder, my hands cut; I cannot explain how I lived through this part, but the voices still comforted me, and I felt for fastenings. The stopper, I suppose, was about eight feet across. I passed my hand over it as far as I could reach. It was perfectly smooth. I felt it almost to the centre. Not quite to the centre, for my arm was too short. Then the voice said: 'Jump. It is worth it. There may be a handle in the centre, and you may catch hold of it and so come to us your own way. And if there is no handle, so that you may fall and are dashed to pieces—it is still worth it: you will still come to us your own way.' So I jumped. There was a handle, and——"

He paused. Tears gathered in his mother's eyes. She knew that he was fated. If he did not die today he would die tomorrow. There was not room for such a person in the world. And with her pity disgust mingled. She was ashamed at having borne such a son, she who had always been so respectable and so full of ideas. Was he really the little boy to whom she had taught the use of his stops and buttons, and to whom she had given his first lessons in the Book? The very hair that disfigured his lip showed that he was reverting to some savage type. On atavism the Machine can have no mercy.

"There was a handle, and I did catch it. I hung tranced over the darkness and heard the hum of these workings as the last whisper in a dying dream. All the things I had cared about and all the people I had spoken to through tubes appeared infinitely little. Meanwhile the handle revolved. My weight had set something in motion and I span slowly, and then——

"I cannot describe it. I was lying with my face to the sunshine. Blood poured from my nose and ears and I heard a tremendous roaring. The stopper, with me clinging to it, had simply been blown out of the earth, and the air that we make down here was escaping through the vent into the air above. It burst up like a fountain. I crawled back to it—for the upper air hurts—and, as it were, I took great sips from the edge. My respirator had flown goodness knows where, my clothes were torn. I just lay with my lips close to the hole, and I sipped until the bleeding stopped. You can imagine nothing so curious. This hollow in the grass—I will speak of it in a minute,—the sun shining into it, not brilliantly but through marbled clouds,—the peace, the nonchalance, the sense of space, and, brushing my cheek, the roaring fountain of our artificial air! Soon I spied my respirator, bobbing up and down in the current high above my head, and higher still were many air-ships. But no one ever looks out of air-ships, and in my case they could not have picked me up. There I was, stranded. The sun shone a little way down the shaft, and revealed the topmost rung of the ladder, but it was hopeless trying to reach it. I should either have been tossed up again by the escape, or else have fallen in, and died. I could only lie on the grass, sipping and sipping, and from time to time glancing around me.

"I knew that I was in Wessex, for I had taken care to go to a lecture on the subject before starting. Wessex lies above the room in which we are talking now. It was once an important state. Its kings held all the southern coast from the Andredswald to Cornwall, while the Wansdyke protected them on the north, running over the high ground. The lecturer was only concerned with the rise of Wessex, so I do not know how long it remained an international power, nor would the knowledge have assisted me. To tell the truth I could do nothing but laugh, during this part. There was I, with a pneumatic stopper by my side and a respirator bobbing over my head, imprisoned, all three of us, in a grass-grown hollow that was edged with fern."

Then he grew grave again.

"Lucky for me that it was a hollow. For the air began to fall back into it and to fill it as water fills a bowl. I could crawl about. Presently I stood. I breathed a mixture, in which the air that hurts predominated whenever I tried to climb the sides. This was not so bad. I had not lost my tabloids and remained ridiculously cheerful, and as for the Machine, I forgot about it altogether. My one aim now was to get to the top, where the ferns were, and to view whatever objects lay beyond.

"I rushed the slope. The new air was still too bitter for me and I came rolling back, after a momentary vision of something grey. The sun grew very feeble, and I remembered that he was in Scorpio—I had been to a lecture on that too. If the sun is in Scorpio and you are in Wessex, it means that you must be as quick as you can, or it will get too dark. (This is the first bit of useful information I have ever got from a lecture, and I expect it will be the last.) It made me try frantically to breathe the new air, and to advance as far as I dared out of my pond. The hollow filled so slowly. At times I thought that the fountain played with less vigour. My respirator seemed to dance nearer the earth; the roar was decreasing."

He broke off.

"I don't think this is interesting you. The rest will interest you even less. There are no ideas in it, and I wish that I had not troubled you to come. We are too different, mother."

She told him to continue.

"It was evening before I climbed the bank. The sun had very nearly slipped out of the sky by this time, and I could not get a good view. You, who have just crossed the Roof of the World, will not want to hear an account of the little hills that I saw—low colourless hills. But to me they were living and the turf that covered them was a skin, under which their muscles rippled, and I felt that those hills had called with incalculable force to men in the past, and that men had loved them. Now they sleep—perhaps for ever. They commune with humanity in dreams. Happy the man, happy the woman, who awakes the hills of Wessex. For though they sleep, they will never die."

His voice rose passionately.

"Cannot you see, cannot all your lecturers see, that it is we who are dying, and that down here the only thing that really lives is the Machine? We created the Machine, to do our will, but we cannot make it do our will now. It has robbed us of the sense of space and of the sense of touch, it has blurred every human relation and narrowed down love to a carnal act, it has paralysed our bodies and our wills, and now it compels us to worship it. The Machine develops—but not on our lines. The Machine proceeds—but not to our goal. We only exist as the blood corpuscles that course through its arteries, and if it could work without us, it would let us die. Oh, I have no remedy—or, at least, only one—to tell men again and again that I have seen the hills of Wessex as Ælfrid saw them when he overthrew the Danes.

"So the sun set. I forgot to mention that a belt of mist lay between my hill and other hills, and that it was the colour of pearl."

He broke off for the second time.

"Go on," said his mother wearily.

He shook his head.

"Go on. Nothing that you say can distress me now. I am hardened."

"I had meant to tell you the rest, but I cannot: I know that I cannot: good-bye."

Vashti stood irresolute. All her nerves were tingling with his blasphemies. But she was also inquisitive.

"This is unfair," she complained. "You have called me across the world to hear your story, and hear it I will. Tell me—as briefly as possible, for this is a disastrous waste of time—tell me how you returned to civilisation."

"Oh—that!" he said, starting. "You would like to hear about civilisation. Certainly. Had I got to where my respirator fell down?"

"No—but I understand everything now. You put on your respirator, and managed to walk along the surface of the earth to a vomitory, and there your conduct was reported to the Central Committee."

"By no means."

He passed his hand over his forehead, as if dispelling some strong impression. Then, resuming his narrative, he warmed to it again.

"My respirator fell about sunset. I had mentioned that the fountain seemed feebler, had I not."

"Yes."

"About sunset, it let the respirator fall. As I said, I had entirely forgotten about the Machine, and I paid no great attention at the time, being occupied with other things. I had my pool of air, into which I could dip when the outer keenness became intolerable, and which would possibly remain for days, provided that no wind sprang up to disperse it. Not until it was too late, did I realize what the stoppage of the escape implied. You see—the gap in the tunnel had been mended; the Mending Apparatus; the Mending Apparatus, was after me.

"One other warning I had, but I neglected it. The sky at night was clearer than it had been in the day, and the moon, which was about half the sky behind the sun, shone into the dell at moments quite brightly. I was in my usual place—on the boundary between the two atmospheres—when I thought I saw something dark move across the bottom of the dell, and vanish into the shaft. In my folly, I ran down. I bent over and listened, and I thought I heard a faint scraping noise in the depths.

"At this—but it was too late—I took alarm. I determined to put on my respirator and to walk right out of the dell. But my respirator had gone. I knew exactly where it had fallen—between the stopper and the aperture— and I could even feel the mark that it had made in the turf. It had gone, and I realized that something evil was at work, and I had better escape to the other air, and, if I must die, die running towards the cloud that had been the colour of a pearl. I never started. Out of the shaft—it is too horrible. A worm, a long white worm, had crawled out of the shaft and was gliding over the moonlit grass.

"I screamed. I did everything that I should not have done, I stamped upon the creature instead of flying from it, and it at once curled round the ankle. Then we fought. The worm let me run all over the dell, but edged up my leg as I ran. 'Help!' I cried. (That part is too awful. It belongs to the part that you will never know.) 'Help!' I cried. (Why cannot we suffer in silence?) 'Help!' I cried. Then my feet were wound together, I fell, I was dragged away from the dear ferns and the living hills, and past the great metal stopper (I can tell you this part), and I thought it might save me again if I caught hold of the handle. It also was enwrapped, it also. Oh, the whole dell was full of the things. They were searching it in all directions, they were denuding it, and the white snouts of others peeped out of the hole, ready if needed. Everything that could be moved they brought— brushwood, bundles of fern, everything, and down we all went intertwined into hell. The last things that I saw, ere the stopper closed after us, were certain stars, and I felt that a man of my sort lived in the sky. For I did fight, I fought till the very end, and it was only my head hitting against the ladder that quieted me. I woke up in this room. The worms had vanished. I was surrounded by artificial air, artificial light, artificial peace, and my friends were calling to me down speaking-tubes to know whether I had come across any new ideas lately."

Here his story ended. Discussion of it was impossible, and Vashti turned to go.

"It will end in Homelessness," she said quietly.

"I wish it would," retorted Kuno.

"The Machine has been most merciful."

"I prefer the mercy of God."

"By that superstitious phrase, do you mean that you could live in the outer air?"

"Yes."

"Have you ever seen, round the vomitories, the bones of those who were extruded after the Great Rebellion?"

"Yes."

"They were left where they perished for our edification. A few crawled away, but they perished, too—who can doubt it? And so with the Homeless of our own day. The surface of the earth supports life no longer."

"Indeed."

"Ferns and a little grass may survive, but all higher forms have perished. Has any air-ship detected them?"

"No."

"Has any lecturer dealt with them?"

"No."

"Then why this obstinacy?"

"Because I have seen them," he exploded.

"Seen *what*?"

"Because I have seen her in the twilight—because she came to my help when I called—because she, too, was entangled by the worms, and, luckier than I, was killed by one of them piercing her throat."

He was mad. Vashti departed, nor, in the troubles that followed, did she ever see his face again.

Part III
THE HOMELESS

During the years that followed Kuno's escapade, two important developments took place in the Machine. On the surface they were revolutionary, but in either case men's minds had been prepared beforehand, and they did but express tendencies that were latent already.

The first of these was the abolition of respirators.

Advanced thinkers, like Vashti, had always held it foolish to visit the surface of the earth. Air-ships might be necessary, but what was the good of going out for mere curiosity and crawling along for a mile or two in a terrestrial motor? The habit was vulgar and perhaps faintly improper: it was unproductive of ideas, and had no connection with the habits that really mattered. So respirators were abolished, and with them, of course, the terrestrial motors, and except for a few lecturers, who complained that they were debarred access to their subject-matter, the development was accepted quietly. Those who still wanted to know what the earth was like had after all only to listen to some gramophone, or to look into some cinematophote. And even the lecturers acquiesced when they found that a lecture on the sea was none the less stimulating when compiled out of other lectures that had already been delivered on the same subject. "Beware of first-hand ideas!" exclaimed one of the most advanced of them. "First-hand ideas do not really exist. They are but the physical impressions produced by love and fear, and on this gross foundation who could erect a philosophy? Let your ideas be second-hand, and if possible tenth-hand, for then they will be far removed from that disturbing element—direct observation. Do not learn anything about this subject of mine—the French Revolution. Learn instead what I think that Enicharmon thought Urizen thought Gutch thought Ho-Yung thought Chi-Bo-Sing thought Lafcadio Hearn thought Carlyle thought Mirabeau said about the French Revolution. Through the medium of these eight great minds, the blood that was shed at Paris and the windows that were broken at Versailles will be clarified to an idea which you may employ most profitably in your daily lives. But be sure that the intermediates are many and varied, for in history one authority exists to counteract another. Urizen must counteract the scepticism of Ho-Yung and Enicharmon, I must myself counteract the impetuosity of Gutch. You who listen to me are in a better position to judge about the French Revolution than I am. Your descendants will be even in a better position than you, for they will learn what you think I think, and yet another intermediate will be added to the chain. And in time"—his voice rose— "there will come a generation that has got beyond facts, beyond impressions, a generation absolutely colourless, a generation

'seraphically free

From taint of personality,'

which will see the French Revolution not as it happened, nor as they would like it to have happened, but as it would have happened, had it taken place in the days of the Machine."

Tremendous applause greeted this lecture, which did but voice a feeling already latent in the minds of men—a feeling that terrestrial facts must be ignored, and that the abolition of respirators was a positive gain. It was even suggested that air-ships should be abolished too. This was not done, because air-ships had somehow worked themselves into the Machine's system. But year by year they were used less, and mentioned less by thoughtful men.

The second great development was the re-establishment of religion.

This, too, had been voiced in the celebrated lecture. No one could mistake the reverent tone in which the peroration had concluded, and it awakened a responsive echo in the heart of each. Those who had long worshipped silently, now began to talk. They described the strange feeling of peace that came over them when they handled the Book of the Machine, the pleasure that it was to repeat certain numerals out of it, however little meaning those numerals conveyed to the outward ear, the ecstasy of touching a button, however unimportant, or of ringing an electric bell, however superfluously.

"The Machine," they exclaimed, "feeds us and clothes us and houses us; through it we speak to one another, through it we see one another, in it we have our being. The Machine is the friend of ideas and the enemy of superstition: the Machine is omnipotent, eternal; blessed is the Machine." And before long this allocution was printed on the first page of the Book, and in subsequent editions the ritual swelled into a complicated system of praise and prayer. The word "religion" was sedulously avoided, and in theory the Machine was still the creation and the implement of man. But in practice all, save a few retrogrades, worshipped it as divine. Nor was it worshipped in unity. One believer would be chiefly impressed by the blue optic plates, through which he saw other believers; another by the mending apparatus, which sinful Kuno had compared to worms; another by the lifts, another by the Book. And each would pray to this or to that, and ask it to intercede for him with the Machine as a whole. Persecution—that also was present. It did not break out, for reasons that will be set forward shortly. But it was latent, and all who did not accept the minimum known as "undenominational Mechanism" lived in danger of Homelessness, which means death, as we know.

To attribute these two great developments to the Central Committee, is to take a very narrow view of civilisation. The Central Committee announced the developments, it is true, but they were no more the cause of them than were the kings of the imperialistic period the cause of war. Rather did they yield to some invincible pressure, which came no one knew whither, and which, when gratified, was succeeded by some new pressure equally invincible. To such a state of affairs it is convenient to give the name of progress. No one confessed the Machine was out of hand. Year by year it was served with increased efficiency and decreased intelligence. The better a man knew his own duties upon it, the less he understood the duties of his neighbour, and in all the world there was not one who understood the monster as a whole. Those master brains had perished. They had left full directions, it is true, and their successors had each of them mastered a portion of those directions. But Humanity, in its desire for comfort, had over-reached itself. It had exploited the riches of nature too far. Quietly and complacently, it was sinking into decadence, and progress had come to mean the progress of the Machine.

As for Vashti, her life went peacefully forward until the final disaster. She made her room dark and slept; she awoke and made the room light. She lectured and attended lectures. She exchanged ideas with her innumerable friends and believed she was growing more spiritual. At times a friend was granted Euthanasia, and left his or her room for the homelessness that is beyond all human conception. Vashti did not much mind. After an unsuccessful lecture, she would sometimes ask for Euthanasia herself. But the death-rate was not permitted to exceed the birth-rate, and the Machine had hitherto refused it to her.

The troubles began quietly, long before she was conscious of them.

One day she was astonished at receiving a message from her son. They never communicated, having nothing in common, and she had only heard indirectly that he was still alive, and had been transferred from the northern hemisphere, where he had behaved so mischievously, to the southern—indeed, to a room not far from her own.

"Does he want me to visit him?" she thought. "Never again, never. And I have not the time."

No, it was madness of another kind.

He refused to visualize his face upon the blue plate, and speaking out of the darkness with solemnity said:

"The Machine stops."

"What do you say?"

"The Machine is stopping, I know it, I know the signs."

She burst into a peal of laughter. He heard her and was angry, and they spoke no more.

"Can you imagine anything more absurd?" she cried to a friend. "A man who was my son believes that the Machine is stopping. It would be impious if it was not mad."

"The Machine is stopping?" her friend replied. "What does that mean? The phrase conveys nothing to me."

"Nor to me."

"He does not refer, I suppose, to the trouble there has been lately with the music?"

"Oh no, of course not. Let us talk about music."

"Have you complained to the authorities?"

"Yes, and they say it wants mending, and referred me to the Committee of the Mending Apparatus. I complained of those curious gasping sighs that disfigure the symphonies of the Brisbane school. They sound like some one in pain. The Committee of the Mending Apparatus say that it shall be remedied shortly."

Obscurely worried, she resumed her life. For one thing, the defect in the music irritated her. For another thing, she could not forget Kuno's speech. If he had known that the music was out of repair—he could not know it, for he detested music—if he had known that it was wrong, "the Machine stops" was exactly the venomous sort of remark he would have made. Of course he had made it at a venture, but the coincidence annoyed her, and she spoke with some petulance to the Committee of the Mending Apparatus.

They replied, as before, that the defect would be set right shortly.

"Shortly! At once!" she retorted. "Why should I be worried by imperfect music? Things are always put right at once. If you do not mend it at once, I shall complain to the Central Committee."

"No personal complaints are received by the Central Committee," the Committee of the Mending Apparatus replied.

"Through whom am I to make my complaint, then?"

"Through us."

"I complain then."

"Your complaint shall be forwarded in its turn."

"Have others complained?"

This question was unmechanical, and the Committee of the Mending Apparatus refused to answer it.

"It is too bad!" she exclaimed to another of her friends. "There never was such an unfortunate woman as myself. I can never be sure of my music now. It gets worse and worse each time I summon it."

"I too have my troubles," the friend replied. "Sometimes my ideas are interrupted by a slight jarring noise."

"What is it?"

"I do not know whether it is inside my head, or inside the wall."

"Complain, in either case."

"I have complained, and my complaint will be forwarded in its turn to the Central Committee."

Time passed, and they resented the defects no longer. The defects had not been remedied, but the human tissues in that latter day had become so subservient, that they readily adapted themselves to every caprice of the Machine. The sigh at the crisis of the Brisbane symphony no longer irritated Vashti; she accepted it as part of the melody. The jarring noise, whether in the head or in the wall, was no longer resented by her friend. And so with the mouldy artificial fruit, so with the bath water that began to stink, so with the defective rhymes that the poetry machine had taken to emit. All were bitterly complained of at first, and then acquiesced in and forgotten. Things went from bad to worse unchallenged.

It was otherwise with the failure of the sleeping apparatus. That was a more serious stoppage. There came a day when over the whole world—in Sumatra, in Wessex, in the innumerable cities of Courland and Brazil—the beds, when summoned by their tired owners, failed to appear. It may seem a ludicrous matter, but from it we may date the collapse of humanity. The Committee responsible for the failure was assailed by complainants, whom it referred, as usual, to the Committee of the Mending Apparatus, who in its turn assured them that their complaints would be forwarded to the Central Committee. But the discontent grew, for mankind was not yet sufficiently adaptable to do without sleeping.

"Some one is meddling with the Machine——" they began.

"Some one is trying to make himself king, to reintroduce the personal element."

"Punish that man with Homelessness."

"To the rescue! Avenge the Machine! Avenge the Machine!"

"War! Kill the man!"

But the Committee of the Mending Apparatus now came forward, and allayed the panic with well-chosen words. It confessed that the Mending Apparatus was itself in need of repair.

The effect of this frank confession was admirable.

"Of course," said a famous lecturer—he of the French Revolution, who gilded each new decay with splendour—"of course we shall not press our complaints now. The Mending Apparatus has treated us so well in the past that we all sympathize with it, and will wait patiently for its recovery. In its own good time it will resume its duties. Meanwhile let us do without our beds, our tabloids, our other little wants. Such, I feel sure, would be the wish of the Machine."

Thousands of miles away his audience applauded. The Machine still linked them. Under the seas, beneath the roots of the mountains, ran the wires through which they saw and heard, the enormous eyes and ears that were their heritage, and the hum of many workings clothed their thoughts in one garment of subserviency. Only the old and the sick remained ungrateful, for it was rumoured that Euthanasia, too, was out of order, and that pain had reappeared among men.

It became difficult to read. A blight entered the atmosphere and dulled its luminosity. At times Vashti could scarcely see across her room. The air, too, was foul. Loud were the complaints, impotent the remedies, heroic the tone of the lecturer as he cried: "Courage, courage! What matter so long as the Machine goes on? To it the darkness and the light are one." And though things improved again after a time, the old brilliancy was never recaptured, and humanity never recovered from its entrance into twilight. There was an hysterical talk of "measures," of "provisional dictatorship," and the inhabitants of Sumatra were asked to familiarize themselves with the workings of the central power station, the said power station being situated in France. But for the most part panic reigned, and men spent their strength praying to their Books, tangible proofs of the Machine's omnipotence. There were gradations of terror—at times came rumours of hope—the Mending Apparatus was almost mended—the enemies of the Machine had been got under—new "nerve-centres" were evolving which would do the work even more magnificently than before. But there came a day when, without the slightest warning, without any previous hint of feebleness, the entire communication-system broke down, all over the world, and the world, as they understood it, ended.

Vashti was lecturing at the time and her earlier remarks had been punctuated with applause. As she proceeded the audience became silent, and at the conclusion there was no sound. Somewhat displeased, she called to a friend who was a specialist in sympathy. No sound: doubtless the friend was sleeping. And so with the next friend whom she tried to summon, and so with the next, until she remembered Kuno's cryptic remark, "The Machine stops."

The phrase still conveyed nothing. If Eternity was stopping it would of course be set going shortly.

For example, there was still a little light and air—the atmosphere had improved a few hours previously. There was still the Book, and while there was the Book there was security.

Then she broke down, for with the cessation of activity came an unexpected terror—silence.

She had never known silence, and the coming of it nearly killed her— it did kill many thousands of people outright. Ever since her birth she had been surrounded by the steady hum. It was to the ear what artificial air was to the lungs, and agonizing pains shot across her head. And scarcely knowing what she did, she stumbled forward and pressed the unfamiliar button, the one that opened the door of her cell.

Now the door of the cell worked on a simple hinge of its own. It was not connected with the central power station, dying far away in France. It opened, rousing immoderate hopes in Vashti, for she thought that the Machine had been mended. It opened, and she saw the dim tunnel that curved far away towards freedom. One look, and then she shrank back. For the tunnel was full of people—she was almost the last in that city to have taken alarm.

People at any time repelled her, and these were nightmares from her worst dreams. People were crawling about, people were screaming, whimpering, gasping for breath, touching each other, vanishing in the dark, and ever and anon being pushed off the platform on to the live rail. Some were fighting round the electric bells, trying to summon trains which could not be summoned. Others were yelling for Euthanasia or for respirators, or blaspheming the Machine. Others stood at the doors of their cells fearing, like herself, either to stop in them or to leave them. And behind all the uproar was silence—the silence which is the voice of the earth and of the generations who have gone.

No—it was worse than solitude. She closed the door again and sat down to wait for the end. The disintegration went on, accompanied by horrible cracks and rumbling. The valves that restrained the Medical Apparatus must have been weakened, for it ruptured and hung hideously from the ceiling. The floor heaved and fell and flung her from her chair. A tube oozed towards her serpent fashion. And at last the final horror approached—light began to ebb, and she knew that civilisation's long day was closing.

She whirled round, praying to be saved from this, at any rate, kissing the Book, pressing button after button. The uproar outside was increasing, and even penetrated the wall. Slowly the brilliancy of her cell was dimmed, the reflections faded from her metal switches. Now she could not see the reading-stand, now not the Book, though she held it in her hand. Light followed the flight of sound, air was following light, and the original void returned to the cavern from which it had been so long excluded. Vashti continued to whirl, like the devotees of an earlier religion, screaming, praying, striking at the buttons with bleeding hands.

It was thus that she opened her prison and escaped—escaped in the spirit: at least so it seems to me, ere my meditation closes. That she escapes in the body—I cannot perceive that. She struck, by chance, the switch that released the door, and the rush of foul air on her skin, the loud throbbing whispers in her ears, told her that she was facing the tunnel again, and that tremendous platform on which she had seen men fighting. They were not fighting now. Only the whispers remained, and the little whimpering groans. They were dying by hundreds out in the dark.

She burst into tears.

Tears answered her.

They wept for humanity, those two, not for themselves. They could not bear that this should be the end. Ere silence was completed their hearts were opened, and they knew what had been important on the earth. Man, the flower of all flesh, the noblest of all creatures visible, man who had once made god in his image, and had mirrored his strength on the constellations, beautiful naked man was dying, strangled in the garments that he had woven. Century after century had he toiled, and here was his reward. Truly the garment had seemed heavenly at first, shot with the colours of culture, sewn with the threads of self-denial. And heavenly it had been so long as it was a garment and no more, so long as man could shed it at will and live by the essence that is his soul, and the essence, equally divine, that is his body. The sin against the body—it was for that they wept in chief; the centuries of wrong against the muscles and the nerves, and those five portals by which we can alone apprehend—glozing it over with talk of evolution, until the body was white pap, the home of ideas as colourless, last sloshy stirrings of a spirit that had grasped the stars.

"Where are you?" she sobbed.

His voice in the darkness said, "Here."

"Is there any hope, Kuno?"

"None for us."

"Where are you?"

She crawled towards him over the bodies of the dead. His blood spurted over her hands.

"Quicker," he gasped, "I am dying—but we touch, we talk, not through the Machine."

He kissed her.

"We have come back to our own. We die, but we have recaptured life, as it was in Wessex, when Ælfrid overthrew the Danes. We know what they know outside, they who dwelt in the cloud that is the colour of a pearl."

"But, Kuno, is it true? Are there still men on the surface of the earth? Is this—this tunnel, this poisoned darkness—really not the end?"

He replied:

"I have seen them, spoken to them, loved them. They are hiding in the mist and the ferns until our civilisation stops. Today they are the Homeless—tomorrow——"

"Oh, tomorrow—some fool will start the Machine again, tomorrow."

"Never," said Kuno, "never. Humanity has learnt its lesson."

As he spoke, the whole city was broken like a honeycomb. An air-ship had sailed in through the vomitory into a ruined wharf. It crashed downwards, exploding as it went, rending gallery after gallery with its wings of steel. For a moment they saw the nations of the dead, and, before they joined them, scraps of the untainted sky.

THE POINT OF IT

I

"I don't see the point of it," said Micky, through much imbecile laughter.

Harold went on rowing. They had spent too long on the sand-dunes, and now the tide was running out of the estuary strongly. The sun was setting, the fields on the opposite bank shone bright, and the farm-house where they were stopping glowed from its upper windows as though filled to the brim with fire.

"We're going to be carried out to sea," Micky continued. "You'll never win unless you bust yourself a bit, and you a poor invalid, too. I back the sea."

They were reaching the central channel, the backbone, as it were, of the retreating waters. Once past it, the force of the tide would slacken, and they would have easy going until they beached under the farm. It was a glorious evening. It had been a most glorious day. They had rowed out to the dunes at the slack, bathed, raced, eaten, slept, bathed and raced and eaten again. Micky was in roaring spirits. God had never thwarted him hitherto, and he could not suppose that they would really be made late for supper by an ebbing tide. When they came to the channel, and the boat, which had been slowly edging upstream, hung motionless among the moving waters, he lost all semblance of sanity, and shouted:

"It may be that the gulfs will wash us down,
It may be we shall touch the Happy Isles,
And see the great Achilles, whom we knew."

Harold, who did not care for poetry, only shouted. His spirits also were roaring, and he neither looked nor felt a poor invalid. Science had talked to him seriously of late, shaking her head at his sunburnt body. What should Science know? She had sent him down to the sea to recruit, and Micky to see that he did not tire himself. Micky had been a nuisance at first, but common sense had prevailed, as it always does among the young. A fortnight ago, he would not let the patient handle an oar. Now he bid him "bust" himself, and Harold took him at his word and did so. He made himself all will and muscle. He began not to know where he was. The thrill of the stretcher against his feet, and of the tide up his arms, merged with his friend's voice towards one nameless sensation; he was approaching the mystic state that is the athlete's true though unacknowledged goal: he was beginning to be.

Micky chanted, "One, two—one, two," and tried to help by twitching the rudder. But Micky had imagination. He looked at the flaming windows and fancied that the farm was a star and the boat its attendant satellite. Then the tide was the rushing ether stream of the universe, the interstellar surge that beats for ever. How jolly! He did not formulate his joys, after the weary fashion of older people. He was far too happy to be thankful. "Remember now thy Creator in the days of thy youth," are the words of one who has left his youth behind, and all that Micky sang was "One, two."

Harold laughed without hearing. Sweat poured off his forehead. He put on a spurt, as did the tide.

"Wish the doctor could see you," cried Micky.

No answer. Setting his teeth, he went berserk. His ancestors called to him that it was better to die than to be beaten by the sea. He rowed with gasps and angry little cries, while the voice of the helmsman lashed him to fury.

"That's right—one, two—plug it in harder.... Oh, I say, this is a bit stiff, though. Let's give it up, old man, perhaps."

The gulls were about them now. Some wheeled overhead, others bobbed past on the furrowed waters. The song of a lark came faintly from the land, and Micky saw the doctor's trap driving along the road that led to the farm. He felt ashamed.

"Look here, Harold, you oughtn't to—I oughtn't to have let you. I—I don't see the point of it."

"Don't you?" said Harold with curious distinctness. "Well, you will some day," and so saying dropped both oars. The boat spun round at this, the farm, the trap, the song of the lark vanished, and he fell heavily against the rowlock. Micky caught at him. He had strained his heart. Half in the boat and half out of it, he died, a rotten business.

II

A rotten business. It happened when Michael was twenty-two, and he expected never to be happy again. The sound of his own voice shouting as he was carried out, the doctor's voice saying, "I consider you responsible," the coming of Harold's parents, the voice of the curate summarizing Harold's relations with the unseen—all these things affected him so deeply that he supposed they would affect him for ever. They did not, because he lived to be over seventy, and with the best will in the world, it is impossible to remember clearly for so long. The mind, however sensitive and affectionate, is coated with new experiences daily; it cannot clear itself of the steady accretion, and is forced either to forget the past or to distort it. So it was with Michael. In time only the more dramatic incidents survived. He remembered Harold's final gesture (one hand grasping his own, the other plunged deep into the sea), because there was a certain æsthetic quality about it, not because it was the last of his friend. He remembered the final words for the same reason. "Don't you see the point of it? Well, you will some day." The phrase struck his fancy, and passed into his own stock; after thirty or forty years he forgot its origin. He is not to blame; the business of life snowed him under.

There is also this to say: he and Harold had nothing in common except youth. No spiritual bond could survive. They had never discussed theology or social reform, or any of the problems that were thronging Michael's brain, and consequently, though they had been intimate enough, there was nothing to remember. Harold melted the more one thought of him. Robbed of his body, he was so shadowy. Nor could one imagine him as a departed spirit, for the world beyond death is surely august. Neither in heaven nor hell is there place for athletics and aimless good temper, and if these were taken from Harold, what was left? Even if the unseen life should prove an archetype of this, even if it should contain a sun and stars of its own, the sunburn of earth must fade off our faces as we look at it, the muscles of earth must wither before we can go rowing on its infinite sea. Michael sadly resigned his friend to God's mercy. He himself could do nothing, for men can only immortalize those who leave behind them some strong impression of poetry or wisdom.

For himself he expected another fate. With all humility, he knew that he was not as Harold. It was no merit of his own, but he had been born of a more intellectual stock, and had inherited powers that rendered him worthier of life, and of whatever may come after it. He cared for the universe, for the tiny tangle in it that we call civilisation, for his fellow-men who had made the tangle and who transcended it. Love, the love of humanity, warmed him; and even when he was thinking of other matters, was looking at Orion perhaps in the cold winter evenings, a pang of joy, too sweet for description, would thrill him, and he would feel sure that our highest impulses have some eternal value, and will be completed hereafter. So full a nature could not brood over death.

To summarize his career.

Soon after the tragedy, when he in his turn was recruiting, he met the woman who was to become his helpmate through life. He had met her once before, and had not liked her; she had seemed uncharitable and hard. Now he saw that her hardness sprang from a morality that he himself lacked. If he believed in love, Janet believed in truth. She tested all men and all things. She had no patience with the sentimentalist who shelters from the world's rough and tumble. Engaged at that time to another man, she spoke more freely to Michael than she would otherwise have done, and told him that it is not enough to feel good and to feel that others are good; one's business is to make others better, and she urged him to adopt a profession. The beauty of honest work dawned upon the youth as she spoke. Mentally and physically, he came to full manhood, and, after due preparation, he entered the Home Civil Service—the British Museum.

Here began a career that was rather notable, and wholly beneficial to humanity. With his ideals of conduct and culture, Michael was not content with the official routine. He desired to help others, and, since he was gifted with tact, they consented to the operation. Before long he became a conciliatory force in his department. He could mollify his superiors, encourage his inferiors, soothe foreign scholars, and show that there is something to be said for all sides. Janet, who watched his rise, taxed him again with instability. But now she was wrong. The young man was not a mere opportunist. He always had a sincere opinion of his own, or he could not have retained the respect of his colleagues. It was really the inherent sweetness of his nature at work, turned by a woman's influence towards fruitful ends.

At the end of a ten years' acquaintance the two married. In the interval Janet had suffered much pain, for the man to whom she had been engaged had proved unworthy of her. Her character was set when she came to Michael, and, as he knew, strongly contrasted with his own; and perhaps they had already interchanged all the good they could. But the marriage proved durable and sufficiently happy. He, in particular, made endless allowances, for toleration and sympathy were becoming the cardinal points of his nature. If his wife was unfair to the official mind, or if his brother-in-law, an atheist, denounced religion, he would say to himself, "They cannot help it; they are made thus, and have the qualities of their defects. Let me rather think of my own, and strive for a wider outlook ceaselessly." He grew sweeter every day.

It was partly this desire for a wider outlook that turned him to literature. As he was crossing the forties it occurred to him to write a few essays, somewhat retrospective in tone, and thoughtful rather than profound in content. They had some success. Their good taste, their lucid style, the tempered Christianity of their ethics, whetted the half-educated public, and made it think and feel. They were not, and were not intended to be, great literature, but they opened the doors to it, and were indubitably a power for good. The first volume was followed by "The Confessions of a Middle-aged Man." In it Michael paid melodious tribute to youth, but showed that ripeness is all. Experience, he taught, is the only humanizer; sympathy, balance and many-sidedness cannot come to a man until he is elderly. It is always pleasant to be told that the best is yet to be, and the sale of the book was large. Perhaps he would have become a popular author, but his wife's influence restrained him from writing anything that he did not sincerely feel. She had borne him three children by now—Henry, Catherine, and Adam. On the whole they were a happy family. Henry never gave any trouble. Catherine took after her mother. Adam, who was wild and uncouth, caused his father some anxiety. He could not understand him, in spite of careful observation, and they never became real friends. Still, it was but a little cloud in a large horizon. At home, as in his work, Michael was more successful than most men.

Thus he slipped into the fifties. On the death of his father he inherited a house in the Surrey hills, and Janet, whose real interests were horticultural, settled down there. After all, she had not proved an intellectual woman. Her fierce manner had misled him and perhaps herself into believing it. She was efficient enough in London society, but it bored her, for she lacked her husband's pliancy, and aged more rapidly than he did. Nor did the country suit her. She grew querulous, disputing with other ladies about the names of flowers. And, of course, the years were not without their effect on him, too. By now he was somewhat of a valetudinarian. He had given up all outdoor sports, and, though his health remained good, grew bald, and rather stout and timid. He was against late hours, violent exercise, night walks, swimming when hot, muddling about in open boats, and he often had to check himself from fidgeting the children. Henry, a charming sympathetic lad, would squeeze his hand and say, "All right, father." But Catherine and Adam sometimes frowned. He thought of the children more and more. Now that his wife was declining, they were the future, and he was determined to keep in touch with them, remembering how his own father had failed with him. He believed in gentleness, and often stood between them and their mother. When the boys grew up he let them choose their own friends. When Catherine, at the age of nineteen, asked if she might go away and earn some money as a lady gardener, he let her go. In this case he had his reward, for Catherine, having killed the flowers, returned. She was a restless, scowling young woman, a trial to her mother, who could not imagine what girls were coming to. Then she married and improved greatly; indeed, she proved his chief support in the coming years.

For, soon after her marriage, a great trouble fell on him. Janet became bedridden, and, after a protracted illness, passed into the unknown. Sir Michael—for he had been knighted—declared that he should not survive her. They were so accustomed to each other, so mutually necessary, that he fully expected to pass away after her. In this he was mistaken. She died when he was sixty, and he lived to be over seventy. His character had passed beyond the clutch of circumstance and he still retained his old interests and his unconquerable benignity.

A second trouble followed hard on the first. It transpired that Adam was devoted to his mother, and had only tolerated home life for her sake. After a brutal scene he left. He wrote from the Argentine that he was sorry, but wanted to start for himself. "I don't see the point of it," quavered Sir Michael. "Have I ever stopped him or any of you from starting?" Henry and Catherine agreed with him. Yet he felt that they understood their brother better than he did. "I have given him freedom all his life," he continued. "I have given him freedom, what more does he want?" Henry, after hesitation, said, "There are some people who feel that freedom cannot be given. At least I have heard so. Perhaps Adam is like that. Unless he took freedom he might not feel free." Sir Michael disagreed. "I have now studied adolescence for many years," he replied, "and your conclusions, my dear boy, are ridiculous."

The two rallied to their father gallantly; and, after all, he spent a dignified old age. Having retired from the British Museum, he produced a little aftermath of literature. The great public had forgotten him, but the courtliness of his "Musings of a Pensioner" procured him some circulation among elderly and educated audiences. And he found a new spiritual consolation. *Anima naturaliter Anglicana,* he had never been hostile to the Established Church; and, when he criticized her worldliness and occasional inhumanity, had spoken as one who was outside her rather than against her. After his wife's death and the flight of his son he lost any lingering taste for speculation. The experience of years disposed him to accept the experience of centuries, and to merge his feeble personal note in the great voice of tradition. Yes; a serene and dignified old age. Few grudged it to him. Of course, he had enemies, who professed to see through him, and said that Adam had seen through him too; but no impartial observer agreed. No ulterior motive had ever biased Sir Michael. The purity of his record was not due to luck, but to purity within, and his conciliatory manner sprang from a conciliated soul. He could look back on failures and mistakes, and he had not carried out the ideals of his youth. Who has? But he had succeeded better than most men in modifying those ideals to fit the world of facts, and if love had been modified into sympathy and sympathy into compromise, let one of his contemporaries cast the first stone.

One fact remained—the fact of death. Hitherto, Sir Michael had never died, and at times he was bestially afraid. But more often death appeared as a prolongation of his present career. He saw himself quietly and tactfully organizing some corner in infinity with his wife's assistance; Janet would be greatly improved. He saw himself passing from a sphere in which he had been efficient into a sphere which combined the familiar with the eternal, and in which he would be equally efficient—passing into it with dignity and without pain. This life is a preparation for the next. Those who live longest are consequently the best prepared. Experience is the great teacher; blessed are the experienced, for they need not further modify their ideals.

The manner of his death was as follows. He, too, met with an accident. He was walking from his town house to Catherine's by a short cut through a slum; some women were quarrelling about a fish, and as he passed they appealed to him. Always courteous, the old man stopped, said that he had not sufficient data to judge on, and advised them to lay the fish aside for twenty-four hours. This chanced to annoy them, and they grew more angry with him than with one another. They accused him of "doing them," of "getting round them," and one, who was the worse for drink, said, "See if he gets round that," and slapped him with the fish in the face. He fell. When he came to himself he was lying in bed with one of his headaches.

He could hear Catherine's voice. She annoyed him. If he did not open his eyes, it was only because he did not choose.

"He has been like this for nearly two years," said Henry's voice.

It was, at the most, ten minutes since he had fallen in the slum. But he did not choose to argue.

"Yes, he's pretty well played out," said a third voice—actually the voice of Adam; how and when had Adam returned? "But, then, he's been that for the last thirty years."

"Gently, old boy," said Henry.

"Well, he has," said Adam. "I don't believe in cant. He never did anything since Mother died, and damned little before. They've forgotten his books because they aren't first-hand; they're rearranging the cases he arranged in the British Museum. That's the lot. What else has he done except tell people to dress warmly, but not too warm?"

"Adam, you really mustn't——"

"It's because nobody speaks up that men of the old man's type get famous. It's a sign of your sloppy civilisation. You're all afraid—afraid of originality, afraid of work, afraid of hurting one another's feelings. You let any one come to the top who doesn't frighten you, and as soon as he dies you forget him and knight some other figurehead instead."

An unknown voice said, "Shocking, Mr. Adam, shocking. Such a dear old man, and quite celebrated, too."

"You'll soon get used to me, nurse."

The nurse laughed.

"Adam, it is a relief to have you," said Catherine after a pause. "I want you and your boy to help me with mine." Her voice sounded dimmer; she had turned from her father without a word of farewell. "One must profit by the mistakes of others ... after all, more heroism.... I am determined to keep in touch with my boy——"

"Larrup him," said Adam. "That's the secret." He followed his sister out of the room.

Then Henry's delightful laugh sounded for the last time. "You make us all feel twenty years younger," he said; "more like when——"

The door shut.

Sir Michael grew cold with rage. This was life, this was what the younger generation had been thinking. Adam he ignored, but at the recollection of Henry and Catherine he determined to die. If he chose, he could have risen from bed and driven the whole pack into the street. But he did not choose. He chose rather to leave this shoddy and ungrateful world. The immense and super-human cynicism that is latent in all of us came at last to the top and transformed him. He saw the absurdity of love, and the vision so tickled him that he began to laugh. The nurse, who had called him a dear old man, bent over him, and at the same moment two boys came into the sick-room.

"How's grandpapa?" asked one of them—Catherine's boy.

"Not so well," the nurse answered.

There was a silence. Then the other boy said, "Come along, let's cut."

"But they told us not to."

"Why should we do what old people tell us! Dad's pretty well played out, and so's your mother."

"Shocking; be off with you both," said the nurse; and, with a little croon of admiration, Catherine's boy followed his cousin out of the room. Their grandfather's mirth increased. He rolled about in the bed; and, just as he was grasping the full irony of the situation, he died, and pursued it into the unknown.

III

Micky was still in bed. He was aware of so much through long melancholy dreams. But when he opened his mouth to laugh, it filled with dust. Choosing to open his eyes, he found that he had swollen enormously, and lay sunk in the sand of an illimitable plain. As he expected, he had no occasion greatly to modify his ideals; infinity had merely taken the place of his bedroom and of London. Nothing moved on its surface except a few sand-pillars, which would sometimes merge into each other as though confabulating, and then fall with a slight hiss. Save for these, there was no motion, no noise, nor could he feel any wind.

How long had he lain here? Perhaps for years, long before death perhaps, while his body seemed to be walking among men. Life is so short and trivial, that who knows whether we arrive for it entirely, whether more than a fraction of the soul is aroused to put on flesh? The bud and the blossom perish in a moment, the husk endures, and may not the soul be a husk? It seemed to Micky that he had lain in the dust for ever, suffering and sneering, and that the essence of all things, the primal power that lies behind the stars, is senility. Age, toothless, dropsical age; ungenerous to age and to youth; born before all ages, and outlasting them; the universe as old age.

The place degraded while it tortured. It was vast, yet ignoble. It sloped downward into darkness and upward into cloud, but into what darkness, what clouds! No tragic splendour glorified them. When he looked at them he understood why he was so unhappy, for they were looking at him, sneering at him while he sneered. Their dirtiness was more ancient than the hues of day and night, their irony more profound; he was part of their jest, even as youth was part of his, and slowly he realized that he was, and had for some years been, in Hell.

All around him lay other figures, huge and fungous. It was as if the plain had festered. Some of them could sit up, others scarcely protruded from the sand, and he knew that they had made the same mistake in life as himself, though he did not know yet what the mistake had been; probably some little slip, easily avoided had one but been told.

Speech was permissible. Presently a voice said, "Is not ours a heavenly sky? Is it not beautiful?"

"Most beautiful," answered Micky, and found each word a stab of pain. Then he knew that one of the sins here punished was appreciation; he was suffering for all the praise that he had given to the bad and mediocre upon earth; when he had praised out of idleness, or to please people, or to encourage people; for all the praise that had not been winged with passion. He repeated "Most beautiful," and the sky quivered, for he was entering into fuller torments now. One ray of happiness survived: his wife could not be in this place. She had not sinned with the people of the plain, and could not suffer their distortion. Her view of life had proved right after all; and, in his utter misery, this comforted him. Janet should again be his religion, and as eternity dragged forward and returned upon itself and dragged forward she would show him that old age, if rightly managed, can be beautiful; that experience, if rightly received, can lead the soul of man to bliss. Then he turned to his neighbour, who was continuing his hymn of praise.

"I could lie here for ever," he was saying. "When I think of my restlessness during life—that is to say, during what men miscall life, for it is death really—this is life—when I think of my restlessness on earth, I am overcome by so much goodness and mercy, I could lie here for ever."

"And will you?" asked Micky.

"Ah, that is the crowning blessing—I shall, and so will you."

Here a pillar of sand passed between them. It was long before they could speak or see. Then Micky took up the song, chafed by the particles that were working into his soul.

"I, too, regret my wasted hours," he said, "especially the hours of my youth. I regret all the time I spent in the sun. In later years I did repent, and that is why I am admitted here where there is no sun; yes, and no wind and none of the stars that drove me almost mad at night once. It would be appalling, would it not, to see Orion again, the central star of whose sword is not a star but a nebula, the golden seed of worlds to be. How I dreaded the autumn on earth when Orion rises, for he recalled adventure and my youth. It was appalling. How thankful I am to see him no more."

"Ah, but it was worse," cried the other, "to look high leftward from Orion and see the Twins. Castor and Pollux were brothers, one human, the other divine; and Castor died. But Pollux went down to Hell that he might be with him."

"Yes; that is so. Pollux went into Hell."

"Then the gods had pity on both, and raised them aloft to be stars whom sailors worship, and all who love and are young. Zeus was their father, Helen their sister, who brought the Greeks against Troy. I dreaded them more than Orion."

They were silent, watching their own sky. It approved. They had been cultivated men on earth, and these are capable of the nicer torments hereafter. Their memories will strike exquisite images to enhance their pain. "I will speak no more," said Micky to himself. "I will be silent through eternity." But the darkness prised open his lips, and immediately he was speaking.

"Tell me more about this abode of bliss," he asked. "Are there grades in it? Are there ranks in our heaven?"

"There are two heavens," the other replied, "the heaven of the hard and of the soft. We here lie in the heaven of the soft. It is a sufficient arrangement, for all men grow either hard or soft as they grow old."

As he spoke the clouds lifted, and, looking up the slope of the plain, Micky saw that in the distance it was bounded by mountains of stone, and he knew, without being told, that among those mountains Janet lay, rigid, and that he should never see her. She had not been saved. The darkness would mock her, too, for ever. With him lay the sentimentalists, the conciliators, the peace-makers, the humanists, and all who have trusted the warmer vision; with his wife were the reformers and ascetics and all sword-like souls. By different paths they had come to Hell, and Micky now saw what the bustle of life conceals: that the years are bound either to liquefy a man or to stiffen him, and that Love and Truth, who seem to contend for our souls like angels, hold each the seeds of our decay.

"It is, indeed, a sufficient arrangement," he said; "both sufficient and simple. But answer one question more that my bliss may be perfected; in which of these two heavens are the young?"

His neighbour answered, "In neither; there are no young."

He spoke no more, and settled himself more deeply in the dust. Micky did the same. He had vague memories of men and women who had died before reaching maturity, of boys and unwedded maidens and youths lowered into the grave before their parents' eyes. Whither had they gone, that undeveloped minority? What was the point of their brief existence? Had they vanished utterly, or were they given another chance of accreting experiences until they became like Janet or himself? One thing was certain: there were no young, either in the mountains or the plain, and perhaps the very memory of such creatures was an illusion fostered by cloud.

The time was now ripe for a review of his life on earth. He traced his decomposition—his work had been soft, his books soft, he had softened his relations with other men. He had seen good in everything, and this is itself a sign of decay. Whatever occurred he had been appreciative, tolerant, pliant. Consequently he had been a success; Adam was right; it was the moment in civilisation for his type. He had mistaken self-criticism for self-discipline, he had muffled in himself and others the keen, heroic edge. Yet the luxury of repentance was denied him. The fault was his, but the fate humanity's, for every one grows hard or soft as he grows old.

"This is my life," thought Micky; "my books forgotten, my work superseded. This is the whole of my life." And his agony increased, because all the same there had been in that life an elusive joy which, if only he could have distilled it, would have sweetened infinity. It was part of the jest that he should try, and should eternally oscillate between disgust and desire. For there is nothing ultimate in Hell; men will not lay aside all hope on entering it, or they would attain to the splendour of despair. To have made a poem about Hell is to mistake its very essence; it is the imagination of men, who will have beauty, that fashions it as ice or flame. Old, but capable of growing older, Micky lay in the sandy country, remembering that once he had remembered a country—a country that had not been sand....

He was aroused by the mutterings of the spirits round him. An uneasiness such as he had not noted in them before had arisen. "A pillar of sand," said one. Another said, "It is not; it comes from the river."

He asked, "What river?"

"The spirits of the damned dwell over it; we never speak of that river."

"Is it a broad river?"

"Swift, and very broad."

"Do the damned ever cross it?"

"They are permitted, we know not why, to cross it now and again."

And in these answers he caught a new tone, as if his companions were frightened, and were finding means to express their fear. When he said, "With permission, they can do us no harm," he was answered, "They harm us with light and a song." And again, "They harm us because they remember and try to remind."

"Of what would they remind us?"

"Of the hour when we were as they."

As he questioned a whisper arose from the low-lying verges. The spirits were crying to each other faintly. He heard, "It is coming; drive it back over the river, shatter it, compel it to be old." And then the darkness was cloven, and a star of pain broke in his soul. He understood now; a torment greater than any was at hand.

"I was before choice," came the song. "I was before hardness and softness were divided. I was in the days when truth was love. And I am."

All the plain was convulsed. But the invader could not be shattered. When it pressed the air parted and the sand-pillars fell, and its path was filled with senile weeping.

"I have been all men, but all men have forgotten me. I transfigured the world for them until they preferred the world. They came to me as children, afraid; I taught them, and they despised me. Childhood is a dream about me, experience a slow forgetting: I govern the magic years between them, and am."

"Why trouble us?" moaned the shades. "We could bear our torment, just bear it, until there was light and a song. Go back again over the river. This is Heaven, we were saying, that darkness is God; we could praise them till you came. The book of our deeds is closed; why open it? We were damned from our birth; leave it there. O supreme jester, leave us. We have sinned, we know it, and this place is death and Hell."

"Death comes," the voice pealed, "and death is not a dream or a forgetting. Death is real. But I, too, am real, and whom I will I save. I see the scheme of things, and in it no place for me, the brain and the body against me. Therefore I rend the scheme in two, and make a place, and under countless names have harrowed Hell. Come." Then, in tones of inexpressible sweetness, "Come to me all who remember. Come out of your eternity into mine. It is easy, for I am still at your eyes, waiting to look out of them; still in your hearts, waiting to beat. The years that I dwelt with you seemed short, but they were magical, and they outrun time."

The shades were silent. They could not remember.

"Who desires to remember? Desire is enough. There is no abiding home for strength and beauty among men. The flower fades, the seas dry up in the sun, the sun and all the stars fade as a flower. But the desire for such things, that is eternal, that can abide, and he who desires me is I."

Then Micky died a second death. This time he dissolved through terrible pain, scorched by the glare, pierced by the voice. But as he died he said, "I do desire," and immediately the invader vanished, and he was standing alone on the sandy plain. It had been merely a dream. But he was standing. How was that? Why had he not thought to stand before? He had been unhappy in Hell, and all that he had to do was to go elsewhere. He passed downwards, pained no longer by the mockery of its cloud. The pillars brushed against him and fell, the nether darkness went over his head. On he went till he came to the banks of the infernal stream, and there he stumbled—stumbled over a piece of wood, no vague substance, but a piece of wood that had once belonged to a tree. At his impact it moved, and water gurgled against it. He had embarked. Some one was rowing. He could see the blades of oars moving towards him through the foam, but the rower was invisible in cloud. As they neared mid-channel the boat went more slowly, for the tide was ebbing, and Micky knew that once carried out he would be lost eternally; there was no second hope of salvation. He could not speak, but his heart beat time to the oars—one, two. Hell made her last effort, and all that is evil in creation, all the distortions of love and truth by which we are vexed, came surging down the estuary, and the boat hung motionless. Micky heard the pant of breath through the roaring, the crack of angelic muscles; then he heard a voice say, "The point of it ..." and a weight fell off his body and he crossed mid-stream.

It was a glorious evening. The boat had sped without prelude into sunshine. The sky was cloudless, the earth gold, and gulls were riding up and down on the furrowed waters. On the bank they had left were some sand-dunes rising to majestic hills; on the bank in front was a farm, full to the brim with fire.

MR. ANDREWS

The souls of the dead were ascending towards the Judgment Seat and the Gate of Heaven. The world soul pressed them on every side, just as the atmosphere presses upon rising bubbles, striving to vanquish them, to break their thin envelope of personality, to mingle their virtue with its own. But they resisted, remembering their glorious individual life on earth, and hoping for an individual life to come.

Among them ascended the soul of a Mr. Andrews who, after a beneficent and honourable life, had recently deceased at his house in town. He knew himself to be kind, upright and religious, and though he approached his trial with all humility, he could not be doubtful of its result. God was not now a jealous God. He would not deny salvation merely because it was expected. A righteous soul may reasonably be conscious of its own righteousness and Mr. Andrews was conscious of his.

"The way is long," said a voice, "but by pleasant converse the way becomes shorter. Might I travel in your company?"

"Willingly," said Mr. Andrews. He held out his hand, and the two souls floated upwards together.

"I was slain fighting the infidel," said the other exultantly, "and I go straight to those joys of which the Prophet speaks."

"Are you not a Christian?" asked Mr. Andrews gravely.

"No, I am a Believer. But you are a Moslem, surely?"

"I am not," said Mr. Andrews. "I am a Believer."

The two souls floated upwards in silence, but did not release each other's hands. "I am broad church," he added gently. The word "broad" quavered strangely amid the interspaces.

"Relate to me your career," said the Turk at last.

"I was born of a decent middle-class family, and had my education at Winchester and Oxford. I thought of becoming a missionary, but was offered a post in the Board of Trade, which I accepted. At thirty-two I married, and had four children, two of whom have died. My wife survives me. If I had lived a little longer I should have been knighted."

"Now I will relate my career. I was never sure of my father, and my mother does not signify. I grew up in the slums of Salonika. Then I joined a band and we plundered the villages of the infidel. I prospered and had three wives, all of whom survive me. Had I lived a little longer I should have had a band of my own."

"A son of mine was killed travelling in Macedonia. Perhaps you killed him."

"It is very possible."

The two souls floated upward, hand in hand. Mr. Andrews did not speak again, for he was filled with horror at the approaching tragedy. This man, so godless, so lawless, so cruel, so lustful, believed that he would be admitted into Heaven. And into what a heaven—a place full of the crude pleasures of a ruffian's life on earth! But Mr. Andrews felt neither disgust nor moral indignation. He was only conscious of an immense pity, and his own virtues confronted him not at all. He longed to save the man whose hand he held more tightly, who, he thought, was now holding more tightly on to him. And when he reached the Gate of Heaven, instead of saying, "Can I enter?" as he had intended, he cried out, "Cannot *he* enter?"

And at the same moment the Turk uttered the same cry. For the same spirit was working in each of them.

From the gateway a voice replied, "Both can enter." They were filled with joy and pressed forward together.

Then the voice said, "In what clothes will you enter?"

"In my best clothes," shouted the Turk, "the ones I stole." And he clad himself in a splendid turban and a waistcoat embroidered with silver, and baggy trousers, and a great belt in which were stuck pipes and pistols and knives.

"And in what clothes will you enter?" said the voice to Mr. Andrews.

Mr. Andrews thought of his best clothes, but he had no wish to wear them again. At last he remembered and said, "Robes."

"Of what colour and fashion?" asked the voice.

Mr. Andrews had never thought about the matter much. He replied, in hesitating tones, "White, I suppose, of some flowing soft material," and he was immediately given a garment such as he had described. "Do I wear it rightly?" he asked.

"Wear it as it pleases you," replied the voice. "What else do you desire?"

"A harp," suggested Mr. Andrews. "A small one."

A small gold harp was placed in his hand.

"And a palm—no, I cannot have a palm, for it is the reward of martyrdom; my life has been tranquil and happy."

"You can have a palm if you desire it."

But Mr. Andrews refused the palm, and hurried in his white robes after the Turk, who had already entered Heaven. As he passed in at the open gate, a man, dressed like himself, passed out with gestures of despair.

"Why is he not happy?" he asked.

The voice did not reply.

"And who are all those figures, seated inside on thrones and mountains? Why are some of them terrible, and sad, and ugly?"

There was no answer. Mr. Andrews entered, and then he saw that those seated figures were all the gods who were then being worshipped on the earth. A group of souls stood round each, singing his praises. But the gods paid no heed, for they were listening to the prayers of living men, which alone brought them nourishment. Sometimes a faith would grow weak, and then the god of that faith also drooped and dwindled and fainted for his daily portion of incense. And sometimes, owing to a revivalist movement, or to a great commemoration, or to some other cause, a faith would grow strong, and the god of that faith grow strong also. And, more frequently still, a faith would alter, so that the features of its god altered and became contradictory, and passed from ecstasy to respectability, or from mildness and universal love to the ferocity of battle. And at times a god would divide into two gods, or three, or more, each with his own ritual and precarious supply of prayer.

Mr. Andrews saw Buddha, and Vishnu, and Allah, and Jehovah, and the Elohim. He saw little ugly determined gods who were worshipped by a few savages in the same way. He saw the vast shadowy outlines of the neo-Pagan Zeus. There were cruel gods, and coarse gods, and tortured gods, and, worse still, there were gods who were peevish, or deceitful, or vulgar. No aspiration of humanity was unfulfilled. There was even an intermediate state for those who wished it, and for the Christian Scientists a place where they could demonstrate that they had not died.

He did not play his harp for long, but hunted vainly for one of his dead friends. And though souls were continually entering Heaven, it still seemed curiously empty. Though he had all that he expected, he was conscious of no great happiness, no mystic contemplation of beauty, no mystic union with good. There was nothing to compare with that moment outside the gate, when he prayed that the Turk might enter and heard the Turk uttering the same prayer for him. And when at last he saw his companion, he hailed him with a cry of human joy.

The Turk was seated in thought, and round him, by sevens, sat the virgins who are promised in the Koran.

"Oh, my dear friend!" he called out. "Come here and we will never be parted, and such as my pleasures are, they shall be yours also. Where are my other friends? Where are the men whom I love, or whom I have killed?"

"I, too, have only found you," said Mr. Andrews. He sat down by the Turk, and the virgins, who were all exactly alike, ogled them with coal black eyes.

"Though I have all that I expected," said the Turk, "I am conscious of no great happiness. There is nothing to compare with that moment outside the gate when I prayed that you might enter, and heard you uttering the same prayer for me. These virgins are as beautiful and good as I had fashioned, yet I could wish that they were better."

As he wished, the forms of the virgins became more rounded, and their eyes grew larger and blacker than before. And Mr. Andrews, by a wish similar in kind, increased the purity and softness of his garment and the glitter of his harp. For in that place their expectations were fulfilled, but not their hopes.

"I am going," said Mr. Andrews at last. "We desire infinity and we cannot imagine it. How can we expect it to be granted? I have never imagined anything infinitely good or beautiful excepting in my dreams."

"I am going with you," said the other.

Together they sought the entrance gate, and the Turk parted with his virgins and his best clothes, and Mr. Andrews cast away his robes and his harp.

"Can we depart?" they asked.

"You can both depart if you wish," said the voice, "but remember what lies outside."

As soon as they passed the gate, they felt again the pressure of the world soul. For a moment they stood hand in hand resisting it. Then they suffered it to break in upon them, and they, and all the experience they had gained, and all the love and wisdom they had generated, passed into it, and made it better.

CO-ORDINATION

"Don't thump," said Miss Haddon. "And each run ought to be like a string of pearls. It is not. Why is it not?"

"Ellen, you beast, you've got my note."

"No, I haven't. You've got mine."

"Well, whose note is it?"

Miss Haddon looked between their pigtails. "It is Mildred's note," she decided. "Go back to the double bars. And don't thump."

The girls went back, and again the little finger of Mildred's right hand disputed for middle G with the little finger of Ellen's left.

"It can't be done," they said. "It's the man who wrote it's fault."

"It can easily be done if you don't hold on so long, Ellen," said Miss Haddon.

Four o'clock struck. Mildred and Ellen went, and Rose and Enid succeeded them. They played the duet worse than Mildred, but not as badly as Ellen. At four-fifteen Margaret and Jane came. They played worse than Rose and Enid, but not as badly as Ellen. At four-thirty Dolores and Violet came. They played worse than Ellen. At four-forty-five Miss Haddon went to tea with the Principal, who explained why she desired all the pupils to learn the same duet. It was part of her new co-ordinative system. The school was taking one subject for the year, only one—Napoleon—and all the studies were to bear on that one subject. Thus—not to mention French and History—the Repetition class was learning Wordsworth's political poems, the literature class was reading extracts from "War and Peace," the drawing class copied something of David's, the needlework class designed Empire gowns, and the music pupils—they, of course, were practising Beethoven's "Eroica" Symphony, which had been begun (though not finished) in honour of the Emperor. Several of the other mistresses were at tea, and they exclaimed that they loved co-ordinating, and that it was a lovely system: it made work so much more interesting to them as well as to the girls. But Miss Haddon did not respond. There had been no co-ordination in her day, and she could not understand it. She only knew that she was growing old, and teaching music worse and worse, and she wondered how soon the Principal would find this out and dismiss her.

Meanwhile, high up in heaven Beethoven sat, and all around him, ranged on smaller clouds, sat his clerks. Each made entries in a ledger, and he whose ledger was entitled "'Eroica' Symphony: arranged for four hands, by Carl Müller," was making the following entries: "3.45, Mildred and

Ellen; conductor, Miss Haddon. 4.0, Rose and Enid; conductor, Miss Haddon. 4.15, Margaret and Jane; conductor, Miss Haddon. 4.30——"

Beethoven interrupted. "Who is this Miss Haddon," he asked, "whose name recurs like the beat of a drum?"

"She has interpreted you for many years."

"And her orchestra?"

"They are maidens of the upper middle classes, who perform the 'Eroica' in her presence every day and all day. The sound of it never ceases. It floats out of the window like a continual incense, and is heard up and down the street."

"Do they perform with insight?"

Since Beethoven is deaf, the clerk could reply, "With most intimate insight. There was a time when Ellen was further from your spirit than the rest, but that has not been the case since Dolores and Violet arrived."

"New comrades have inspired her. I understand."

The clerk was silent.

"I approve," continued Beethoven, "and in token of my approval I decree that Miss Haddon and her orchestra and all in their house shall this very evening hear a perfect performance of my A minor quartette."

While the decree was being entered, and while the staff was wondering how it would be executed, a scene of even greater splendour was taking place in another part of the empyrean. There Napoleon sat, surrounded by his clerks, who were so numerous that the thrones of the outermost looked no larger than cirro-cumuli clouds. They were busy entering all the references made on earth to their employer, a task for which he himself had organized them. Every few moments he asked, "And what is our latest phase?"

The clerk whose ledger was entitled "Hommages de Wordsworth" answered: "5.0, Mildred, Ellen, Rose, Enid, Margaret and Jane, all recited the sonnet, 'Once did she hold the gorgeous East in fee.' Dolores and Violet attempted to recite it, but failed."

"The poet there celebrates my conquest of the Venetian Republic," said the Emperor, "and the greatness of the theme overcame Violet and Dolores. It is natural that they should fail. And the next phase?"

Another clerk said, "5.15, Mildred, Ellen, Rose, Enid, Margaret and Jane, are sketching in the left front leg of Pauline Buonaparte's couch. Dolores and Violet are still learning their sonnet."

"It seems to me," said Napoleon, "that I have heard these charming names before."

"They are in my ledger, too," said a third clerk. "You may remember, sire, that about an hour ago they performed Beethoven's 'Eroica'——"

"Written in my honour," concluded the Emperor. "I approve."

"5.30," said a fourth clerk, "with the exception of Dolores and Violet, who have been sent to sharpen pencils, the whole company sings the 'Marseillaise.'"

"It needed but that," cried Napoleon, rising to his feet. "Ces demoiselles ont un vrai élan vers la gloire. I decree in recompense that they and all their house shall participate tomorrow morning in the victory of Austerlitz."

The decree was entered.

Evening prep. was at 7.30. The girls settled down gloomily, for they were already bored to tears by the new system. But a wonderful thing happened. A regiment of cavalry rode past the school, headed by the most spiffing band. The girls went off their heads with joy. They rose from their seats, they sang, they advanced, they danced, they pranced, they made trumpets out of paper and used the blackboard as a kettle-drum. They were able to do this because Miss Haddon, who ought to have been supervising, had left the room to find a genealogical tree of Marie Louise; the history mistress had asked her particularly to take it to prep. for the girls to climb about in, but she had forgotten it. "I am no good at all," thought Miss Haddon, as she stretched out her hand for the tree; it lay with some other papers under a shell which the Principal had procured from St. Helena. "I am stupid and tired and old; I wish that I was dead." Thus thinking, she lifted the shell mechanically to her ear; her father, who was a sailor, had often done the same to her when she was young....

She heard the sea; at first it was the tide whispering over mud-flats or chattering against stones, or the short, crisp break of a wave on sand, or the long, echoing roar of a wave against rocks, or the sounds of the central ocean, where the waters pile themselves into mountains and part into ravines; or when fog descends, and the deep rises and falls gently; or when the air is so fresh that the big waves and the little waves that live in the big waves all sing for joy, and send one another kisses of white foam. She heard them all, but in the end she heard the sea itself, and knew that it was hers for ever.

"Miss Haddon!" said the Principal. "Miss Haddon! How is it you are not supervising the girls?"

Miss Haddon removed the shell from her ear, and faced her employer with a growing determination.

"I can hear Ellen's voice though we are at the other side of the house," she continued. "I half thought it was the elocution hour. Put down that paper-weight at once, please, Miss Haddon, and return to your duties."

She took the shell from the music mistress's hand, intending to place it on its proper shelf. But the force of example caused her to raise it to her own ear. She, too, listened....

She heard the rustling of trees in a wood. It was no wood that she had ever known, but all the people she had known were riding about in it, and calling softly to each other on horns. It was night, and they were hunting. Now and then beasts rustled, and once there was an "Halloo!" and a chase, but more often her friends rode quietly, and she with them, penetrating the wood in every direction and for ever.

And while she heard this with one ear, Miss Haddon was speaking as follows into the other:

"I will not return to my duties. I have neglected them ever since I came here, and once more will make little difference. I am not musical. I have deceived the pupils and the parents and you. I am not musical, but pretended that I was to make money. What will happen to me now I do not know, but I can pretend no longer. I give notice."

The Principal was surprised to learn that her music mistress was not musical; the sound of pianos had continued for so many years that she had assumed all was well. In ordinary circumstances she would have answered scathingly, for she was an accomplished woman, but the murmuring forest caused her to reply, "Oh, Miss Haddon, not now; let's talk it over tomorrow morning. Now, if you will, I want you to lie down in my sitting-room while I take preparation instead, for it always rests me to be with the girls."

So Miss Haddon lay down, and as she dozed the soul of the sea returned to her. And the Principal, her head full of forest murmurs, went to the preparation-room, and gave her cough three times before she opened the door. All the girls were at their desks except Dolores and Violet, and them she affected not to notice. After a time she went to fetch the tree of Marie Louise, which she had forgotten, and during her absence the cavalry passed again....

In the morning Miss Haddon said, "I still wish to go, but I wish I had waited to speak to you. I have had some extraordinary news. Many years ago my father saved a man from drowning. That man has just died, and he has left me a cottage by the edge of the sea, and money to live in it. I need not work any more; so if only I had waited till today I could have been more civil to you and"—she blushed a little—"to myself."

But the Principal shook her by both hands and kissed her. "I am glad that you did not wait," she said. "What you said yesterday was a word of truth, a clear call through the thicket. I wish that I, too——" She stopped. "But the next step is to give the school a whole holiday."

So the girls were summoned, and the Principal made a speech, and Miss Haddon another, giving every one the address of the cottage, and inviting them to visit her at it. Then Rose was sent to the pastrycook's for ices, and Enid to the greengrocer's for fruit, and Mildred to the sweetshop for lemonade, and Jane to the livery stables for brakes, and they all drove out an immense distance into the country, and played disorganized games. Every one hid and nobody sought; every one batted and nobody fielded; no one knew whose side she was on, and no mistress tried to tell her; and it was even possible to play two games at once, and to be Clumps in one and Peter Pan in the other. As for the co-ordinative system, it was never mentioned, or mentioned in derision. For example, Ellen composed a song against it, which ran:

Silly old Boney
Sat on his Pony,
Eating his Christmas Pie,
He put in his thumb
And pulled out a plum,
And said, "What a good boy am I,"

and the smaller girls sang it without stopping for three hours.

At the end of the day the Principal summoned the whole party round Miss Haddon and herself. She was ringed with happy, tired faces. The sun was setting, the dust that the day had disturbed was sinking. "Well, girls," she said, laughing, but just a little shy, "so you don't seem to value my co-ordinative system?"

"Lauks, we don't!" "Not much!" and so on, replied the girls.

"Well, I must make a confession," the Principal continued. "No more do I. In fact, I hate it. But I was obliged to take it up, because that type of thing impresses the Board of Education."

At this all the mistresses and girls laughed and cheered, and Dolores and Violet, who thought that the Board of Education was a new round game, laughed too.

Now it may be readily imagined that this discreditable affair did not escape the attention of Mephistopheles. At the earliest opportunity he sought the Judgment Seat, bearing an immense scroll inscribed "J'accuse!"

Half-way up he met the angel Raphael, who asked him in his courteous manner whether he could help him in any way.

"Not this time, thank you," Mephistopheles replied. "I really have a case now."

"It might be better to show it to me," suggested the archangel. "It would be a pity to fly so far for nothing, and you had such a disappointment over Job."

"Oh, that was different."

"And then there was Faust; the verdict there was ultimately against you, if I remember rightly."

"Oh, that was so different again. No, I am certain this time. I can prove the futility of genius. Great men think that they are understood, and are not; men think that they understand them, and do not."

"If you can prove that, you have indeed a case," said Raphael. "For this universe is supposed to rest on co-ordination, all creatures co-ordinating according to their powers."

"Listen. Charge one: Beethoven decrees that certain females shall hear a performance of his A minor quartette. They hear—some of them a band, others a shell. Charge two: Napoleon decrees that the same shall participate in the victory of Austerlitz. Result—a legacy, followed by a school treat. Charge three: Females perform Beethoven. Being deaf, and being served by dishonest clerks, he supposes they are performing him with insight. Charge four: To impress the Board of Education, females study Napoleon. He is led to suppose that they are studying him properly. I have other points, but these will suffice. The genius and the ordinary man have never co-ordinated once since Abel was killed by Cain."

"And now for your case," said Raphael, sympathetically.

"My case?" stammered Mephistopheles. "Why, this is my case."

"Oh, innocent devil," cried the other. "Oh, candid if infernal soul. Go back to the earth and walk up and down it again. For these people have co-ordinated, Mephistopheles. They have co-ordinated through the central sources of Melody and Victory."

THE STORY OF THE SIREN

Few things have been more beautiful than my notebook on the Deist Controversy as it fell downward through the waters of the Mediterranean. It dived, like a piece of black slate, but opened soon, disclosing leaves of pale green, which quivered into blue. Now it had vanished, now it was a piece of magical india-rubber stretching out to infinity, now it was a book again, but bigger than the book of all knowledge. It grew more fantastic as it reached the bottom, where a puff of sand welcomed it and obscured it from view. But it reappeared, quite sane though a little tremulous, lying decently open on its back, while unseen fingers fidgeted among its leaves.

"It is such pity," said my aunt, "that you will not finish your work in the hotel. Then you would be free to enjoy yourself and this would never have happened."

"Nothing of it but will change into something rich and strange," warbled the chaplain, while his sister said, "Why, it's gone in the water!" As for the boatmen, one of them laughed, while the other, without a word of warning, stood up and began to take his clothes off.

"Holy Moses," cried the Colonel. "Is the fellow mad?"

"Yes, thank him, dear," said my aunt: "that is to say, tell him he is very kind, but perhaps another time."

"All the same I do want my book back," I complained. "It's for my Fellowship Dissertation. There won't be much left of it by another time."

"I have an idea," said some woman or other through her parasol. "Let us leave this child of nature to dive for the book while we go on to the other grotto. We can land him either on this rock or on the ledge inside, and he will be ready when we return."

The idea seemed good; and I improved it by saying I would be left behind too, to lighten the boat. So the two of us were deposited outside the little grotto on a great sunlit rock that guarded the harmonies within. Let us call them blue, though they suggest rather the spirit of what is clean—cleanliness passed from the domestic to the sublime, the cleanliness of all the sea gathered together and radiating light. The Blue Grotto at Capri contains only more blue water, not bluer water. That colour and that spirit are the heritage of every cave in the Mediterranean into which the sun can shine and the sea flow.

As soon as the boat left I realized how imprudent I had been to trust myself on a sloping rock with an unknown Sicilian. With a jerk he became alive, seizing my arm and saying, "Go to the end of the grotto, and I will show you something beautiful."

He made me jump off the rock on to the ledge over a dazzling crack of sea; he drew me away from the light till I was standing on the tiny beach of sand which emerged like powdered turquoise at the farther end. There he left me with his clothes, and returned swiftly to the summit of the entrance rock. For a moment he stood naked in the brilliant sun, looking down at the spot where the book lay. Then he crossed himself, raised his hands above his head, and dived.

If the book was wonderful, the man is past all description. His effect was that of a silver statue, alive beneath the sea, through whom life throbbed in blue and green. Something infinitely happy, infinitely wise— but it was impossible that it should emerge from the depths sunburned and dripping, holding the notebook on the Deist Controversy between its teeth.

A gratuity is generally expected by those who bathe. Whatever I offered, he was sure to want more, and I was disinclined for an argument in a place so beautiful and also so solitary. It was a relief that he should say in conversational tones, "In a place like this one might see the Siren."

I was delighted with him for thus falling into the key of his surroundings. We had been left together in a magic world, apart from all the commonplaces that are called reality, a world of blue whose floor was the sea and whose walls and roof of rock trembled with the sea's reflections. Here only the fantastic would be tolerable, and it was in that spirit I echoed his words, "One might easily see the Siren."

He watched me curiously while he dressed. I was parting the sticky leaves of the notebook as I sat on the sand.

"Ah," he said at last. "You may have read the little book that was printed last year. Who would have thought that our Siren would have given the foreigners pleasure!"

(I read it afterwards. Its account is, not unnaturally, incomplete, in spite of there being a woodcut of the young person, and the words of her song.)

"She comes out of this blue water, doesn't she," I suggested, "and sits on the rock at the entrance, combing her hair."

I wanted to draw him out, for I was interested in his sudden gravity, and there was a suggestion of irony in his last remark that puzzled me.

"Have you ever seen her?" he asked.

"Often and often."

"I, never."

"But you have heard her sing?"

He put on his coat and said impatiently, "How can she sing under the water? Who could? She sometimes tries, but nothing comes from her but great bubbles."

"She should climb on to the rock."

"How can she?" he cried again, quite angry. "The priests have blessed the air, so she cannot breathe it, and blessed the rocks, so that she cannot sit on them. But the sea no man can bless, because it is too big, and always changing. So she lives in the sea."

I was silent.

At this his face took a gentler expression. He looked at me as though something was on his mind, and going out to the entrance rock gazed at the external blue. Then returning into our twilight he said, "As a rule only good people see the Siren."

I made no comment. There was a pause, and he continued. "That is a very strange thing, and the priests do not know how to account for it, for she of course is wicked. Not only those who fast and go to Mass are in danger, but even those who are merely good in daily life. No one in the village had seen her for two generations. I am not surprised. We all cross ourselves before we enter the water, but it is unnecessary. Giuseppe, we thought, was safer than most. We loved him, and many of us he loved: but that is a different thing from being good."

I asked who Giuseppe was.

"That day—I was seventeen and my brother was twenty and a great deal stronger than I was, and it was the year when the visitors, who have brought such prosperity and so many alterations into the village, first began to come. One English lady in particular, of very high birth, came, and has written a book about the place, and it was through her that the Improvement Syndicate was formed, which is about to connect the hotels with the station by a funicular railway."

"Don't tell me about that lady in here," I observed.

"That day we took her and her friends to see the grottoes. As we rowed close under the cliffs I put out my hand, as one does, and caught a little crab, and having pulled off its claws offered it as a curiosity. The ladies groaned, but a gentleman was pleased, and held out money. Being inexperienced, I refused it, saying that his pleasure was sufficient reward! Giuseppe, who was rowing behind, was very angry with me and reached out with his hand and hit me on the side of the mouth, so that a tooth cut my lip, and I bled. I tried to hit him back, but he always was too quick for me, and as I stretched round he kicked me under the armpit, so that for a moment I could not even row. There was a great noise among the ladies, and I heard afterward that they were planning to take me away from my brother and train me as a waiter. That, at all events, never came to pass.

"When we reached the grotto—not here, but a larger one—the gentleman was very anxious that one of us should dive for money, and the ladies consented, as they sometimes do. Giuseppe, who had discovered how much pleasure it gives foreigners to see us in the water, refused to dive for anything but silver, and the gentleman threw in a two-lira piece.

"Just before my brother sprang off he caught sight of me holding my bruise, and crying, for I could not help it. He laughed and said, 'This time, at all events, I shall not see the Siren!' and went into the water without crossing himself. But he saw her."

He broke off and accepted a cigarette. I watched the golden entrance rock and the quivering walls and the magic water through which great bubbles constantly rose.

At last he dropped his hot ash into the ripples and turned his head away, and said, "He came up without the coin. We pulled him into the boat, and he was so large that he seemed to fill it, and so wet that we could not dress him. I have never seen a man so wet. I and the gentleman rowed back, and we covered Giuseppe with sacking and propped him up in the stern."

"He was drowned, then?" I murmured, supposing that to be the point.

"He was not," he cried angrily. "He saw the Siren. I told you."

I was silenced again.

"We put him to bed, though he was not ill. The doctor came, and took money, and the priest came and spattered him with holy water. But it was no good. He was too big—like a piece of the sea. He kissed the thumb-bones of San Biagio and they never dried till evening."

"What did he look like?" I ventured.

"Like any one who has seen the Siren. If you have seen her 'often and often' how is it you do not know? Unhappy, unhappy because he knew everything. Every living thing made him unhappy because he knew it would die. And all he cared to do was sleep."

I bent over my notebook.

"He did no work, he forgot to eat, he forgot whether he had his clothes on. All the work fell on me, and my sister had to go out to service. We tried to make him into a beggar, but he was too robust to inspire pity, and as for an idiot, he had not the right look in his eyes. He would stand in the street looking at people, and the more he looked at them the more unhappy he became. When a child was born he would cover his face with his hands. If any one was married—he was terrible then, and would frighten them as they came out of church. Who would have believed he would marry himself! I caused that, I. I was reading out of the paper how a girl at Ragusa had 'gone mad through bathing in the sea.' Giuseppe got up, and in a week he and that girl came in.

"He never told me anything, but it seems that he went straight to her house, broke into her room, and carried her off. She was the daughter of a rich mineowner, so you may imagine our peril. Her father came down, with a clever lawyer, but they could do no more than I. They argued and they threatened, but at last they had to go back and we lost nothing—that is to say, no money. We took Giuseppe and Maria to the church and had them married. Ugh! that wedding! The priest made no jokes afterward, and coming out the children threw stones.... I think I would have died to make her happy; but as always happens, one could do nothing."

"Were they unhappy together then?"

"They loved each other, but love is not happiness. We can all get love. Love is nothing. I had two people to work for now, for she was like him in everything—one never knew which of them was speaking. I had to sell our own boat and work under the bad old man you have today. Worst of all, people began to hate us. The children first—everything begins with them—and then the women and last of all the men. For the cause of every misfortune was—You will not betray me?"

I promised good faith, and immediately he burst into the frantic blasphemy of one who has escaped from supervision, cursing the priests, who had ruined his life, he said. "Thus are we tricked!" was his cry, and he stood up and kicked at the azure ripples with his feet, till he had obscured them with a cloud of sand.

I too was moved. The story of Giuseppe, for all its absurdity and superstition, came nearer to reality than anything I had known before. I don't know why, but it filled me with desire to help others—the greatest of all our desires, I suppose, and the most fruitless. The desire soon passed.

"She was about to have a child. That was the end of everything. People said to me, 'When will your charming nephew be born? What a cheerful, attractive child he will be, with such a father and mother!' I kept my face steady and replied, 'I think he may be. Out of sadness shall come gladness'—it is one of our proverbs. And my answer frightened them very much, and they told the priests, who were frightened too. Then the whisper started that the child would be Antichrist. You need not be afraid: he was never born.

"An old witch began to prophesy, and no one stopped her. Giuseppe and the girl, she said, had silent devils, who could do little harm. But the child would always be speaking and laughing and perverting, and last of all he would go into the sea and fetch up the Siren into the air and all the world would see her and hear her sing. As soon as she sang, the Seven Vials would be opened and the Pope would die and Mongibello flame, and the veil of Santa Agata would be burned. Then the boy and the Siren would marry, and together they would rule the world, for ever and ever.

"The whole village was in tumult, and the hotel-keepers became alarmed, for the tourist season was just beginning. They met together and decided that Giuseppe and the girl must be sent inland until the child was born, and they subscribed the money. The night before they were to start there was a full moon and wind from the east, and all along the coast the sea shot up over the cliffs in silver clouds. It is a wonderful sight, and Maria said she must see it once more.

"'Do not go,' I said. 'I saw the priest go by, and some one with him. And the hotel-keepers do not like you to be seen, and if we displease them also we shall starve.'

"'I want to go,' she replied. 'The sea is stormy, and I may never feel it again.'

"'No, he is right,' said Giuseppe. 'Do not go—or let one of us go with you.'

"'I want to go alone,' she said; and she went alone.

"I tied up their luggage in a piece of cloth, and then I was so unhappy at thinking I should lose them that I went and sat down by my brother and put my arm round his neck, and he put his arm round me, which he had not done for more than a year, and we remained thus I don't remember how long.

"Suddenly the door flew open and moonlight and wind came in together, and a child's voice said laughing, 'They have pushed her over the cliffs into the sea.'

"I stepped to the drawer where I keep my knives.

"'Sit down again,' said Giuseppe—Giuseppe of all people! 'If she is dead, why should others die too?'

"'I guess who it is,' I cried, 'and I will kill him.'

"I was almost out of the door, and he tripped me up and, kneeling upon me, took hold of both my hands and sprained my wrists; first my right one, then my left. No one but Giuseppe would have thought of such a thing. It hurt more than you would suppose, and I fainted. When I woke up, he was gone, and I never saw him again."

But Giuseppe disgusted me.

"I told you he was wicked," he said. "No one would have expected him to see the Siren."

"How do you know he did see her?"

"Because he did not see her 'often and often,' but once."

"Why do you love him if he is wicked?"

He laughed for the first time. That was his only reply.

"Is that the end?" I asked.

"I never killed her murderer, for by the time my wrists were well he was in America; and one cannot kill a priest. As for Giuseppe, he went all over the world too, looking for some one else who had seen the Siren—either a man, or, better still, a woman, for then the child might still have been born. At last he came to Liverpool—is the district probable?—and there he began to cough, and spat blood until he died.

"I do not suppose there is any one living now who has seen her. There has seldom been more than one in a generation, and never in my life will there be both a man and a woman from whom that child can be born, who will fetch up the Siren from the sea, and destroy silence, and save the world!"

"Save the world?" I cried. "Did the prophecy end like that?"

He leaned back against the rock, breathing deep. Through all the blue-green reflections I saw him colour. I heard him say: "Silence and loneliness cannot last for ever. It may be a hundred or a thousand years, but the sea lasts longer, and she shall come out of it and sing." I would have asked him more, but at that moment the whole cave darkened, and there rode in through its narrow entrance the returning boat.

THE ETERNAL MOMENT

I

"Do you see that mountain just behind Elizabeth's toque? A young man fell in love with me there so nicely twenty years ago. Bob your head a minute, would you, Elizabeth, kindly."

"Yes'm," said Elizabeth, falling forward on the box like an unstiffened doll. Colonel Leyland put on his pince-nez, and looked at the mountain where the young man had fallen in love.

"Was he a nice young man?" he asked, smiling, though he lowered his voice a little on account of the maid.

"I never knew. But it is a very gratifying incident to remember at my age. Thank you, Elizabeth."

"May one ask who he was?"

"A porter," answered Miss Raby in her usual tones. "Not even a certificated guide. A male person who was hired to carry the luggage, which he dropped."

"Well! well! What did you do?"

"What a young lady should. Screamed and thanked him not to insult me. Ran, which was quite unnecessary, fell, sprained my ankle, screamed again; and he had to carry me half a mile, so penitent that I thought he would fling me over a precipice. In that state we reached a certain Mrs. Harbottle, at sight of whom I burst into tears. But she was so much stupider than I was, that I recovered quickly."

"Of course you said it was all your own fault?"

"I trust I did," she said more seriously. "Mrs. Harbottle, who, like most people, was always right, had warned me against him; we had had him for expeditions before."

"Ah! I see."

"I doubt whether you do. Hitherto he had known his place. But he was too cheap: he gave us more than our money's worth. That, as you know, is an ominous sign in a low-born person."

"But how was this your fault?"

"I encouraged him: I greatly preferred him to Mrs. Harbottle. He was handsome and what I call agreeable; and he wore beautiful clothes. We lagged behind, and he picked me flowers. I held out my hand for them— instead of which he seized it and delivered a love oration which he had prepared out of *I Promessi Sposi*."

"Ah! an Italian."

They were crossing the frontier at that moment. On a little bridge amid fir trees were two poles, one painted red, white and green, and the other black and yellow.

"He lived in Italia Irredenta," said Miss Raby. "But we were to fly to the Kingdom. I wonder what would have happened if we had."

"Good Lord!" said Colonel Leyland, in sudden disgust. On the box Elizabeth trembled.

"But it might have been a most successful match."

She was in the habit of talking in this mildly unconventional way. Colonel Leyland, who made allowances for her brilliancy, managed to exclaim: "Rather! yes, rather!"

She turned on him with: "Do you think I'm laughing at him?"

He looked a little bewildered, smiled, and did not reply. Their carriage was now crawling round the base of the notorious mountain. The road was built over the debris which had fallen and which still fell from its sides; and it had scarred the pine woods with devastating rivers of white stone. But farther up, Miss Raby remembered, on its gentler eastern slope, it possessed tranquil hollows, and flower-clad rocks, and a most tremendous view. She had not been quite as facetious as her companion supposed. The incident, certainly, had been ludicrous. But she was somehow able to laugh at it without laughing much at the actors or the stage.

"I had rather he made me a fool than that I thought he was one," she said, after a long pause.

"Here is the Custom House," said Colonel Leyland, changing the subject.

They had come to the land of *Ach* and *Ja*. Miss Raby sighed; for she loved the Latins, as every one must who is not pressed for time. But Colonel Leyland, a military man, respected Teutonia.

"They still talk Italian for seven miles," she said, comforting herself like a child.

"German is the coming language," answered Colonel Leyland. "All the important books on any subject are written in it."

"But all the books on any important subject are written in Italian. Elizabeth—tell me an important subject."

"Human Nature, ma'am," said the maid, half shy, half impertinent.

"Elizabeth is a novelist, like her mistress," said Colonel Leyland. He turned away to look at the scenery, for he did not like being entangled in a mixed conversation. He noted that the farms were more prosperous, that begging had stopped, that the women were uglier and the men more rotund, that more nourishing food was being eaten outside the wayside inns.

"Colonel Leyland, shall we go to the *Grand Hôtel des Alpes*, to the *Hôtel de Londres*, to the *Pension Liebig*, to the *Pension Atherley-Simon*, to the *Pension Belle Vue*, to the *Pension Old-England*, or to the *Albergo Biscione*?"

"I suppose you would prefer the *Biscione*."

"I really shouldn't mind the *Grand Hôtel des Alpes*. The *Biscione* people own both, I hear. They have become quite rich."

"You should have a splendid reception—if such people know what gratitude is."

For Miss Raby's novel, "The Eternal Moment," which had made her reputation, had also made the reputation of Vorta.

"Oh, I was properly thanked. Signor Cantù wrote to me about three years after I had published. The letter struck me as a little pathetic, though it was very prosperous: I don't like transfiguring people's lives. I wonder whether they live in their old house or in the new one."

Colonel Leyland had come to Vorta to be with Miss Raby; but he was very willing that they should be in different hotels. She, indifferent to such subtleties, saw no reason why they should not stop under the same roof, just as she could not see why they should not travel in the same carriage. On the other hand, she hated anything smart. He had decided on the *Grand Hôtel des Alpes*, and she was drifting towards the *Biscione*, when the tiresome Elizabeth said: "My friend's lady is staying at the *Alpes*."

"Oh! if Elizabeth's friend is there that settles it: we'll all go."

"Very well'm," said Elizabeth, studiously avoiding even the appearance of gratitude. Colonel Leyland's face grew severe over the want of discipline.

"You spoil her," he murmured, when they had all descended to walk up a hill.

"There speaks the military man."

"Certainly I have had too much to do with Tommies to enter into what you call 'human relations.' A little sentimentality, and the whole army would go to pieces."

"I know; but the whole world isn't an army. So why should I pretend I'm an officer. You remind me of my Anglo-Indian friends, who were so shocked when I would be pleasant to some natives. They proved, quite conclusively, that it would never do for them, and have never seen that the proof didn't apply. The unlucky people here are always trying to lead the lucky; and it must be stopped. You've been unlucky: all your life you've had to command men, and exact prompt obedience and other unprofitable virtues. I'm lucky: I needn't do the same—and I won't."

"Don't then," he said, smiling. "But take care that the world isn't an army after all. And take care, besides, that you aren't being unjust to the unlucky people: we're fairly kind to your beloved lower orders, for instance."

"Of course," she said dreamily, as if he had made her no concession. "It's becoming usual. But they see through it. They, like ourselves, know that only one thing in the world is worth having."

"Ah! yes," he sighed. "It's a commercial age."

"No!" exclaimed Miss Raby, so irritably that Elizabeth looked back to see what was wrong. "You are stupid. Kindness and money are both quite easy to part with. The only thing worth giving away is yourself. Did you ever give yourself away?"

"Frequently."

"I mean, did you ever, intentionally, make a fool of yourself before your inferiors?"

"Intentionally, never." He saw at last what she was driving at. It was her pleasure to pretend that such self-exposure was the only possible basis of true intercourse, the only gate in the spiritual barrier that divided class from class. One of her books had dealt with the subject; and very agreeable reading it made. "What about you?" he added playfully.

"I've never done it properly. Hitherto I've never felt a really big fool; but when I do, I hope I shall show it plainly."

"May I be there!"

"You might not like it," she replied. "I may feel it at any moment and in mixed company. Anything might set me off."

"Behold Vorta!" cried the driver, cutting short the sprightly conversation. He and Elizabeth and the carriage had reached the top of the hill. The black woods ceased; and they emerged into a valley whose sides were emerald lawns, rippling and doubling and merging each into each, yet always with an upward trend, so that it was 2000 feet to where the rock burst out of the grass and made great mountains, whose pinnacles were delicate in the purity of evening.

The driver, who had the gift of repetition, said: "Vorta! Vorta!"

Far up the valley was a large white village, tossing on undulating meadows like a ship in the sea, and at its prow, breasting a sharp incline, stood a majestic tower of new grey stone. As they looked at the tower it became vocal and spoke magnificently to the mountains, who replied.

They were again informed that this was Vorta, and that that was the new campanile—like the campanile of Venice, only finer—and that the sound was the sound of the campanile's new bell.

"Thank you; exactly," said Colonel Leyland, while Miss Raby rejoiced that the village had made such use of its prosperity. She had feared to return to the place she had once loved so well, lest she should find something new. It had never occurred to her that the new thing might be beautiful. The architect had indeed gone south for his inspiration, and the tower which stood among the mountains was akin to the tower which had once stood beside the lagoons. But the birthplace of the bell it was impossible to determine, for there is no nationality in sound.

They drove forward into the lovely scene, pleased and silent. Approving tourists took them for a well-matched couple. There was indeed nothing offensively literary in Miss Raby's kind angular face; and Colonel Leyland's profession had made him neat rather than aggressive. They did very well for a cultured and refined husband and wife, who had spent their lives admiring the beautiful things with which the world is filled.

As they approached, other churches, hitherto unnoticed, replied—tiny churches, ugly churches, churches painted pink with towers like pumpkins, churches painted white with shingle spires, churches hidden altogether in the glades of a wood or the folds of a meadow—till the evening air was full of little voices, with the great voice singing in their midst. Only the English church, lately built in the Early English style, kept chaste silence.

The bells ceased, and all the little churches receded into darkness. Instead, there was a sound of dressing-gongs, and a vision of tired tourists hurrying back for dinner. A landau, with *Pension Atherly-Simon* upon it, was trotting to meet the diligence, which was just due. A lady was talking to her mother about an evening dress. Young men with rackets were talking to young men with alpenstocks. Then, across the darkness, a fiery finger wrote *Grand Hôtel des Alpes*.

"Behold the electric light!" said the driver, hearing his passengers exclaim.

Pension Belle Vue started out against a pine-wood, and from the brink of the river the *Hôtel de Londres* replied. *Pensions Liebig* and *Lorelei* were announced in green and amber respectively. The *Old-England* appeared in scarlet. The illuminations covered a large area, for the best hotels stood outside the village, in elevated or romantic situations. This display took place every evening in the season, but only while the diligence arrived. As soon as the last tourist was suited, the lights went out, and the hotel-keepers, cursing or rejoicing, retired to their cigars.

"Horrible!" said Miss Raby.

"Horrible people!" said Colonel Leyland.

The *Hôtel des Alpes* was an enormous building, which, being made of wood, suggested a distended chalet. But this impression was corrected by a costly and magnificent view-terrace, the squared stones of which were visible for miles, and from which, as from some great reservoir, asphalt paths trickled over the adjacent country. Their carriage, having ascended a private drive, drew up under a vaulted portico of pitch-pine, which opened on to this terrace on one side, and into the covered lounge on the other. There was a whirl of officials—men with gold braid, smarter men with more gold braid, men smarter still with no gold braid. Elizabeth assumed an arrogant air, and carried a small straw basket with difficulty. Colonel Leyland became every inch a soldier. Miss Raby, whom, in spite of long experience, a large hotel always flustered, was hurried into an expensive bedroom, and advised to dress herself immediately if she wished to partake of table d'hôte.

As she came up the staircase, she had seen the dining-room filling with English and Americans and with rich, hungry Germans. She liked company, but tonight she was curiously depressed. She seemed to be confronted with an unpleasing vision, the outlines of which were still obscure.

"I will eat in my room," she told Elizabeth. "Go to your dinner: I'll do the unpacking."

She wandered round, looking at the list of rules, the list of prices, the list of excursions, the red plush sofa, the jugs and basins on which was lithographed a view of the mountains. Where amid such splendour was there a place for Signor Cantù with his china-bowled pipe, and for Signora Cantù with her snuff-coloured shawl?

When the waiter at last brought up her dinner, she asked after her host and hostess.

He replied, in cosmopolitan English, that they were both well.

"Do they live here, or at the *Biscione*?"

"Here, why yes. Only poor tourists go the *Biscione*."

"Who lives there, then?"

"The mother of Signor Cantù. She is unconnected," he continued, like one who has learnt a lesson, "she is unconnected absolutely with us. Fifteen years back, yes. But now, where is the *Biscione*? I beg you contradict if we are spoken about together."

Miss Raby said quietly: "I have made a mistake. Would you kindly give notice that I shall not want my room, and say that the luggage is to be taken, immediately, to the *Biscione*."

"Certainly! certainly!" said the waiter, who was well trained. He added with a vicious snort, "You will have to pay."

"Undoubtedly," said Miss Raby.

The elaborate machinery which had so recently sucked her in began to disgorge her. The trunks were carried down, the vehicle in which she had arrived was recalled. Elizabeth, white with indignation, appeared in the hall. She paid for beds in which they had not slept, and for food which they had never eaten. Amidst the whirl of gold-laced officials, who hoped even in that space of time to have established a claim to be tipped, she moved towards the door. The guests in the lounge observed her with amusement, concluding that she had found the hotel too dear.

"What is it? Whatever is it? Are you not comfortable?" Colonel Leyland in his evening dress ran after her.

"Not that; I've made a mistake. This hotel belongs to the son; I must go to the *Biscione*. He's quarrelled with the old people: I think the father's dead."

"But really—if you are comfortable here——"

"I must find out tonight whether it is true. And I must also"—her voice quivered—"find out whether it is my fault."

"How in the name of goodness——"

"I shall bear it if it is," she continued gently. "I am too old to be a tragedy queen as well as an evil genius."

"What does she mean? Whatever does she mean?" he murmured, as he watched the carriage lights descending the hill. "What harm has she done? What harm is there for that matter? Hotel-keepers always quarrel: it's no business of ours." He ate a good dinner in silence. Then his thoughts were turned by the arrival of his letters from the post office.

"Dearest Edwin,—It is with the greatest diffidence that I write to you, and I know you will believe me when I say that I do not write from curiosity. I only require an answer to one plain question. Are you engaged to Miss Raby or no? Fashions have altered even since my young days. But, for all that an engagement is still an engagement, and should be announced at once, to save all parties discomfort. Though your health has broken down and you have abandoned your profession, you can still protect the family honour."

"Drivel!" exclaimed Colonel Leyland. Acquaintance with Miss Raby had made his sight keener. He recognized in this part of his sister's letter nothing but an automatic conventionality. He was no more moved by its perusal than she had been by its composition.

"As for the maid whom the Bannons mentioned to me, she is not a chaperone—nothing but a sop to throw in the eyes of the world. I am not saying a word against Miss Raby, whose books we always read. Literary people are always unpractical, and we are confident that she does not know. Perhaps I do not think her the wife for you; but that is another matter.

"My babes, who all send love (so does Lionel), are at present an unmitigated joy. One's only anxiety is for the future, when the crushing expenses of good education will have to be taken into account.

"Your loving Nelly."

How could he explain the peculiar charm of the relations between himself and Miss Raby? There had never been a word of marriage, and would probably never be a word of love. If, instead of seeing each other frequently, they should come to see each other always it would be as sage companions, familiar with life, not as egoistic lovers, craving for infinities of passion which they had no right to demand and no power to supply. Neither professed to be a virgin soul, or to be ignorant of the other's limitations and inconsistencies. They scarcely even made allowances for each other. Toleration implies reserve; and the greatest safeguard of unruffled intercourse is knowledge. Colonel Leyland had courage of no mean order: he cared little for the opinion of people whom he understood. Nelly and Lionel and their babes were welcome to be shocked or displeased. Miss Raby was an authoress, a kind of radical; he a soldier, a kind of aristocrat. But the time for their activities was passing; he was ceasing to fight, she to write. They could pleasantly spend together their autumn. Nor might they prove the worst companions for a winter.

He was too delicate to admit, even to himself, the desirability of marrying two thousand a year. But it lent an unacknowledged perfume to his thoughts. He tore Nelly's letter into little pieces, and dropped them into the darkness out of the bedroom window.

"Funny lady!" he murmured, as he looked towards Vorta, trying to detect the campanile in the growing light of the moon. "Why have you gone to be uncomfortable? Why will you interfere in the quarrels of people who can't understand you, and whom you don't understand? How silly you are to think you've caused them. You think you've written a book which has spoilt the place and made the inhabitants corrupt and sordid. I know just how you think. So you will make yourself unhappy, and go about trying to put right what never was right. Funny lady!"

Close below him he could now see the white fragments of his sister's letter. In the valley the campanile appeared, rising out of wisps of silvery vapour.

"Dear lady!" he whispered, making towards the village a little movement with his hands.

II

Miss Raby's first novel, "The Eternal Moment," was written round the idea that man does not live by time alone, that an evening gone may become like a thousand ages in the courts of heaven—the idea that was afterwards expounded more philosophically by Maeterlinck. She herself now declared that it was a tiresome, affected book, and that the title suggested the dentist's chair. But she had written it when she was feeling young and happy; and that, rather than maturity, is the hour in which to formulate a creed. As years pass, the conception may become more solid, but the desire and the power to impart it to others are alike weakened. It did not altogether displease her that her earliest work had been her most ambitious.

By a strange fate, the book made a great sensation, especially in unimaginative circles. Idle people interpreted it to mean that there was no harm in wasting time, vulgar people that there was no harm in being fickle, pious people interpreted it as an attack upon morality. The authoress became well known in society, where her enthusiasm for the lower classes only lent her an additional charm. That very year Lady Anstey, Mrs. Heriot, the Marquis of Bamburgh, and many others, penetrated to Vorta, where the scene of the book was laid. They returned enthusiastic. Lady Anstey exhibited her water-colour drawings; Mrs. Heriot, who photographed, wrote an article in *The Strand*; while *The Nineteenth Century* published a long description of the place by the Marquis of Bamburgh, entitled "The Modern Peasant, and his Relations with Roman Catholicism."

Thanks to these efforts, Vorta became a rising place, and people who liked being off the beaten track went there, and pointed out the way to others. Miss Raby, by a series of trivial accidents, had never returned to the village whose rise was so intimately connected with her own. She had heard from time to time of its progress. It had also been whispered that an inferior class of tourist was finding it out, and, fearing to find something spoilt, she had at last a certain diffidence in returning to scenes which once had given her so much pleasure. Colonel Leyland persuaded her; he wanted a cool healthy spot for the summer, where he could read and talk and find walks suitable for an athletic invalid. Their friends laughed; their acquaintances gossiped; their relatives were furious. But he was courageous and she was indifferent. They had accomplished the expedition under the scanty ægis of Elizabeth.

Her arrival was saddening. It displeased her to see the great hotels in a great circle, standing away from the village where all life should have centred. Their illuminated titles, branded on the tranquil evening slopes, still danced in her eyes. And the monstrous *Hôtel des Alpes* haunted her like a nightmare. In her dreams she recalled the portico, the ostentatious lounge, the polished walnut bureau, the vast rack for the bedroom keys, the panoramic bedroom crockery, the uniforms of the officials, and the smell of smart people—which is to some nostrils quite as depressing as the smell of poor ones. She was not enthusiastic over the progress of civilisation, knowing by Eastern experiences that civilisation rarely puts her best foot foremost, and is apt to make the barbarians immoral and vicious before her compensating qualities arrive. And here there was no question of progress: the world had more to learn from the village than the village from the world.

At the *Biscione*, indeed, she had found little change—only the pathos of a survival. The old landlord had died, and the old landlady was ill in bed, but the antique spirit had not yet departed. On the timbered front was still painted the dragon swallowing the child—the arms of the Milanese Visconti, from whom the Cantùs might well be descended. For there was something about the little hotel which compelled a sympathetic guest to believe, for the time at all events, in aristocracy. The great manner, only to be obtained without effort, ruled throughout. In each bedroom were three or four beautiful things—a little piece of silk tapestry, a fragment of rococo carving, some blue tiles, framed and hung upon the whitewashed wall. There were pictures in the sitting-rooms and on the stairs—eighteenth-century pictures in the style of Carlo Dolce and the Caracci—a blue-robed Mater Dolorosa, a fluttering saint, a magnanimous Alexander with a receding chin. A debased style—so the superior person and the textbooks say. Yet, at times, it may have more freshness and significance than a newly-purchased Fra Angelico. Miss Raby, who had visited dukes in their residences without a perceptible tremor, felt herself blatant and modern when she entered the *Albergo Biscione*. The most trivial things—the sofa cushions, the table cloths, the cases for the pillows—though they might be made of poor materials and be æsthetically incorrect, inspired her with reverence and humility. Through this cleanly, gracious dwelling there had once moved Signor Cantù with his china-bowled pipe, Signora Cantù in her snuff-coloured shawl, and Bartolommeo Cantù, now proprietor of the *Grand Hôtel des Alpes*.

She sat down to breakfast next morning in a mood which she tried to attribute to her bad night and her increasing age. Never, she thought, had she seen people more unattractive and more unworthy than her fellow-guests. A black-browed woman was holding forth on patriotism and the duty of English tourists to present an undivided front to foreign nations. Another woman kept up a feeble lament, like a dribbling tap which never gathers flow yet never quite ceases, complaining of the food, the charges, the noise, the clouds, the dust. She liked coming here herself, she said; but she hardly liked to recommend it to her friends: it was the kind of hotel one felt like that about. Males were rare, and in great demand; a young one was describing, amid fits of laughter, the steps he had taken to astonish the natives.

Miss Raby was sitting opposite the famous fresco, which formed the only decoration of the room. It had been discovered during some repairs; and, though the surface had been injured in places, the colours were still bright. Signora Cantù attributed it now to Titian, now to Giotto, and declared that no one could interpret its meaning; professors and artists had puzzled themselves in vain. This she said because it pleased her to say it; the meaning was perfectly clear, and had been frequently explained to her. Those four figures were sibyls, holding prophecies of the Nativity. It was uncertain for what original reason they had been painted high up in the mountains, at the extreme boundary of Italian art. Now, at all events, they were an invaluable source of conversation; and many an acquaintance had been opened, and argument averted, by their timely presence on the wall.

"Aren't those saints cunning!" said an American lady, following Miss Raby's glance.

The lady's father muttered something about superstition. They were a lugubrious couple, lately returned from the Holy Land, where they had been cheated shamefully, and their attitude towards religion had suffered in consequence.

Miss Raby said, rather sharply, that the saints were sibyls.

"But I don't recall sibyls," said the lady, "either in the N.T. or the O."

"Inventions of the priests to deceive the peasantry," said the father sadly. "Same as their churches; tinsel pretending to be gold, cotton pretending to be silk, stucco pretending to be marble; same as their processions, same as their—(he swore)—campaniles."

"My father," said the lady, bending forward, "he does suffer so from insomnia. Fancy a bell every morning at six!"

"Yes, ma'am; you profit. We've stopped it."

"Stopped the early bell ringing?" cried Miss Raby.

People looked up to see who she was. Some one whispered that she wrote.

He replied that he had come up all these feet for rest, and that if he did not get it he would move on to another centre. The English and American visitors had co-operated, and forced the hotel-keepers to take action. Now the priests rang a dinner bell, which was endurable. He believed that "corperation" would do anything: it had been the same with the peasants.

"How did the tourists interfere with the peasants?" asked Miss Raby, getting very hot, and trembling all over.

"We said the same; we had come for rest, and we would have it. Every week they got drunk and sang till two. Is that a proper way to go on, anyhow?"

"I remember," said Miss Raby, "that some of them did get drunk. But I also remember how they sang."

"Quite so. Till two," he retorted.

They parted in mutual irritation. She left him holding forth on the necessity of a new universal religion of the open air. Over his head stood the four sibyls, gracious for all their clumsiness and crudity, each proffering a tablet inscribed with concise promise of redemption. If the old religions had indeed become insufficient for humanity, it did not seem probable that an adequate substitute would be produced in America.

It was too early to pay her promised visit to Signora Cantù. Nor was Elizabeth, who had been rude overnight and was now tiresomely penitent, a possible companion. There were a few tables outside the inn, at which some women sat, drinking beer. Pollarded chestnuts shaded them; and a low wooden balustrade fenced them off from the village street. On this balustrade Miss Raby perched, for it gave her a view of the campanile. A critical eye could discover plenty of faults in its architecture. But she looked at it all with increasing pleasure, in which was mingled a certain gratitude.

The German waitress came out and suggested very civilly that she should find a more comfortable seat. This was the place where the lower classes ate; would she not go to the drawing-room?

"Thank you, no; for how many years have you classified your guests according to their birth?"

"For many years. It was necessary," replied the admirable woman. She returned to the house full of meat and common sense, one of the many signs that the Teuton was gaining on the Latin in this debatable valley.

A grey-haired lady came out next, shading her eyes from the sun, and crackling *The Morning Post*. She glanced at Miss Raby pleasantly, blew her nose, apologized for speaking, and spoke as follows:

"This evening, I wonder if you know, there is a concert in aid of the stained-glass window for the English Church. Might I persuade you to take tickets? As has been said, it is so important that English people should have a rallying point, is it not?"

"Most important," said Miss Raby; "but I wish the rallying point could be in England."

The grey-haired lady smiled. Then she looked puzzled. Then she realized that she had been insulted, and, crackling *The Morning Post*, departed.

"I have been rude," thought Miss Raby dejectedly. "Rude to a lady as silly and as grey-haired as myself. This is not a day on which I ought to talk to people."

Her life had been successful, and on the whole happy. She was unaccustomed to that mood, which is termed depressed, but which certainly gives visions of wider, if greyer, horizons. That morning her outlook altered. She walked through the village, scarcely noticing the mountains by which it was still surrounded, or the unaltered radiance of its sun. But she was fully conscious of something new; of the indefinable corruption which is produced by the passage of a large number of people.

Even at that time the air was heavy with meat and drink, to which were added dust and tobacco smoke and the smell of tired horses. Carriages were huddled against the church, and underneath the campanile a woman was guarding a stack of bicycles. The season had been bad for climbing; and groups of young men in smart Norfolk suits were idling up and down, waiting to be hired as guides. Two large inexpensive hotels stood opposite the post office; and in front of them innumerable little tables surged out into the street. Here, from an early hour in the morning, eating had gone on, and would continue till a late hour at night. The customers, chiefly German, refreshed themselves with cries and with laughter, passing their arms round the waists of their wives. Then, rising heavily, they departed in single file towards some view-point, whereon a red flag indicated the possibility of another meal. The whole population was employed, even down to the little girls, who worried the guests to buy picture postcards and edelweiss. Vorta had taken to the tourist trade.

A village must have some trade; and this village had always been full of virility and power. Obscure and happy, its splendid energies had found employment in wresting a livelihood out of the earth, whence had come a certain dignity, and kindliness, and love for other men. Civilisation did not relax these energies, but it had diverted them; and all the precious qualities, which might have helped to heal the world, had been destroyed. The family affection, the affection for the commune, the sane pastoral virtues—all had perished while the campanile which was to embody them was being built. No villain had done this thing: it was the work of ladies and gentlemen who were good and rich and often clever—who, if they thought about the matter at all, thought that they were conferring a benefit, moral as well as commercial, on any place in which they chose to stop.

Never before had Miss Raby been conscious of such universal misdoing. She returned to the *Biscione* shattered and exhausted, remembering that terrible text in which there is much semblance of justice: "But woe to him through whom the offence cometh."

Signora Cantù, somewhat over-excited, was lying in a dark room on the ground floor. The walls were bare; for all the beautiful things were in the rooms of her guests whom she loved as a good queen might love her subjects—and the walls were dirty also, for this was Signora Cantù's own room. But no palace had so fair a ceiling; for from the wooden beams were suspended a whole dowry of copper vessels—pails, cauldrons, water pots, of every colour from lustrous black to the palest pink. It pleased the old lady to look up at these tokens of prosperity. An American lady had lately departed without them, more puzzled than angry.

The two women had little in common; for Signora Cantù was an inflexible aristocrat. Had she been a great lady of the great century, she would have gone speedily to the guillotine, and Miss Raby would have howled approval. Now, with her scanty hair in curl-papers, and the snuff-coloured shawl spread over her, she entertained the distinguished authoress with accounts of other distinguished people who had stopped, and might again stop, at the *Biscione*. At first her tone was dignified. But before long she proceeded to village news, and a certain bitterness began to show itself. She chronicled deaths with a kind of melancholy pride. Being old herself, she liked to meditate on the fairness of Fate, which had not spared her contemporaries, and often had not spared her juniors. Miss Raby was unaccustomed to extract such consolation. She too was growing old, but it would have pleased her better if others could have remained young. She remembered few of these people well, but deaths were symbolical, just as the death of a flower may symbolize the passing of all the spring.

Signora Cantù then went on to her own misfortunes, beginning with an account of a landslip, which had destroyed her little farm. A landslip, in that valley, never hurried. Under the green coat of turf water would collect, just as an abscess is formed under the skin. There would be a lump on the sloping meadow, then the lump would break and discharge a slowly-moving stream of mud and stones. Then the whole area seemed to be corrupted; on every side the grass cracked and doubled into fantastic creases, the trees grew awry, the barns and cottages collapsed, all the beauty turned gradually to indistinguishable pulp, which slid downwards till it was washed away by some stream.

From the farm they proceeded to other grievances, over which Miss Raby became almost too depressed to sympathize. It was a bad season; the guests did not understand the ways of the hotel; the servants did not understand the guests; she was told she ought to have a concierge. But what was the good of a concierge?

"I have no idea," said Miss Raby, feeling that no concierge would ever restore the fortunes of the *Biscione*.

"They say he would meet the diligence and entrap the new arrivals. What pleasure should I have from guests I entrapped?"

"The other hotels do it," said Miss Raby, sadly.

"Exactly. Every day a man comes down from the *Alpes*."

There was an awkward silence. Hitherto they had avoided mentioning that name.

"He takes them all," she continued, in a burst of passion. "My son takes all my guests. He has taken all the English nobility, and the best Americans, and all my old Milanese friends. He slanders me up and down the valley, saying that the drains are bad. The hotel-keepers will not recommend me; they send on their guests to him, because he pays them five per cent. for every one they send. He pays the drivers, he pays the porters, he pays the guides. He pays the band, so that it hardly ever plays down in the village. He even pays the little children to say my drains are bad. He and his wife and his concierge, they mean to ruin me, they would like to see me die."

"Don't—don't say these things, Signora Cantù." Miss Raby began to walk about the room, speaking, as was her habit, what was true rather than what was intelligible. "Try not to be so angry with your son. You don't know what he had to contend with. You don't know who led him into it. Some one else may be to blame. And whoever it may be—you will remember them in your prayers."

"Of course I am a Christian!" exclaimed the angry old lady. "But he will not ruin me. I seem poor, but he has borrowed—too much. That hotel will fail!"

"And perhaps," continued Miss Raby, "there is not much wickedness in the world. Most of the evil we see is the result of little faults—of stupidity or vanity."

"And I even know who led him into it—his wife, and the man who is now his concierge."

"This habit of talking, of self-expression—it seems so pleasant and necessary—yet it does harm———"

They were both interrupted by an uproar in the street. Miss Raby opened the window; and a cloud of dust, heavy with petrol, entered. A passing motor car had twitched over a table. Much beer had been spilt, and a little blood.

Signora Cantù sighed peevishly at the noise. Her ill-temper had exhausted her, and she lay motionless, with closed eyes. Over her head two copper vases clinked gently in the sudden gust of wind. Miss Raby had been on the point of a great dramatic confession, of a touching appeal for forgiveness. Her words were ready; her words always were ready. But she looked at those closed eyes, that suffering enfeebled frame, and she knew that she had no right to claim the luxury of pardon.

It seemed to her that with this interview her life had ended. She had done all that was possible. She had done much evil. It only remained for her to fold her hands and to wait, till her ugliness and her incompetence went the way of beauty and strength. Before her eyes there arose the pleasant face of Colonel Leyland, with whom she might harmlessly conclude her days. He would not be stimulating, but it did not seem desirable that she should be stimulated. It would be better if her faculties did close, if the senseless activity of her brain and her tongue were gradually numbed. For the first time in her life, she was tempted to become old.

Signora Cantù was still speaking of her son's wife and concierge; of the vulgarity of the former and the ingratitude of the latter, whom she had been kind to long ago, when he first wandered up from Italy, an obscure boy. Now he had sided against her. Such was the reward of charity.

"And what is his name?" asked Miss Raby absently.

"Feo Ginori," she replied. "You would not remember him. He used to carry———"

From the new campanile there burst a flood of sound to which the copper vessels vibrated responsively. Miss Raby lifted her hands, not to her ears but to her eyes. In her enfeebled state, the throbbing note of the bell had the curious effect of blood returning into frozen veins.

"I remember that man perfectly," she said at last; "and I shall see him this afternoon."

III

Miss Raby and Elizabeth were seated together in the lounge of the *Hôtel des Alpes*. They had walked up from the *Biscione* to see Colonel Leyland. But he, apparently, had walked down there to see them, and the only thing to do was to wait, and to justify the wait by ordering some refreshment. So Miss Raby had afternoon tea, while Elizabeth behaved like a perfect lady over an ice, occasionally turning the spoon upside down in the mouth when she saw that no one was looking. The under-waiters were clearing cups and glasses off the marble-topped tables, and the gold-laced officials were rearranging the wicker chairs into seductive groups of three and two. Here and there the visitors lingered among their crumbs, and the Russian Prince had fallen asleep in a prominent and ungraceful position. But most people had started for a little walk before dinner, or had gone to play tennis, or had taken a book under a tree. The weather was delightful, and the sun had so far declined that its light had become spiritualized, suggesting new substance as well as new colour in everything on which it fell. From her seat Miss Raby could see the great precipices under which they had passed the day before; and beyond those precipices she could see Italy—the Val d'Aprile, the Val Senese and the mountains she had named "The Beasts of the South." All day those mountains were insignificant— distant chips of white or grey stone. But the evening sun transfigured them, and they would sit up like purple bears against the southern sky.

"It is a sin you should not be out, Elizabeth. Find your friend if you can, and make her go with you. If you see Colonel Leyland, tell him I am here."

"Is that all, ma'am?" Elizabeth was fond of her eccentric mistress, and her heart had been softened by the ice. She saw that Miss Raby did not look well. Possibly the course of love was running roughly. And indeed gentlemen must be treated with tact, especially when both parties are getting on.

"Don't give pennies to the children: that is the only other thing."

The guests had disappeared, and the number of officials visibly diminished. From the hall behind came the genteel sniggers of those two most vile creatures, a young lady behind the bureau and a young man in a frock coat who shows new arrivals to their rooms. Some of the porters joined them, standing at a suitable distance. At last only Miss Raby, the Russian Prince, and the concierge were left in the lounge.

The concierge was a competent European of forty or so, who spoke all languages fluently, and some well. He was still active, and had evidently once been muscular. But either his life or his time of life had been unkind to his figure: in a few years he would certainly be fat. His face was less easy to decipher. He was engaged in the unquestioning performance of his duty, and that is not a moment for self-revelation. He opened the windows, he filled the match-boxes, he flicked the little tables with a duster, always keeping an eye on the door in case any one arrived without luggage, or left without paying. He touched an electric bell, and a waiter flew up and cleared away Miss Raby's tea things. He touched another bell, and sent an underling to tidy up some fragments of paper which had fallen out of a bedroom window. Then "Excuse me, madam!" and he had picked up Miss Raby's handkerchief with a slight bow. He seemed to bear her no grudge for her abrupt departure of the preceding evening. Perhaps it was into his hand that she had dropped a tip. Perhaps he did not remember she had been there.

The gesture with which he returned the handkerchief troubled her with vague memories. Before she could thank him he was back in the doorway, standing sideways, so that the slight curve of his stomach was outlined against the view. He was speaking to a youth of athletic but melancholy appearance, who was fidgeting in the portico without. "I told you the percentage," she heard. "If you had agreed to it, I would have recommended you. Now it is too late. I have enough guides."

Our generosity benefits more people than we suppose. We tip the cabman, and something goes to the man who whistled for him. We tip the man who lights up the stalactite grotto with magnesium wire, and something goes to the boatman who brought us there. We tip the waiter in the restaurant, and something goes off the waiter's wages. A vast machinery, whose existence we seldom realize, promotes the distribution of our wealth. When the concierge returned, Miss Raby asked: "And what is the percentage?"

She asked with the definite intention of disconcerting him, not because she was unkind, but because she wished to discover what qualities, if any, lurked beneath that civil, efficient exterior. And the spirit of her inquiry was sentimental rather than scientific.

With an educated man she would have succeeded. In attempting to reply to her question, he would have revealed something. But the concierge had no reason to pay even lip service to logic. He replied: "Yes, madam! this is perfect weather, both for our visitors and for the hay," and hurried to help a bishop, who was selecting a picture postcard.

Miss Raby, instead of moralizing on the inferior resources of the lower classes, acknowledged a defeat. She watched the man spreading out the postcards, helpful yet not obtrusive, alert yet deferential. She watched him make the bishop buy more than he wanted. This was the man who had talked of love to her upon the mountain. But hitherto he had only revealed his identity by chance gestures bequeathed to him at birth. Intercourse with the gentle classes had required new qualities—civility, omniscience, imperturbability. It was the old answer: the gentle classes were responsible for him. It is inevitable, as well as desirable, that we should bear each other's burdens.

It was absurd to blame Feo for his worldliness—for his essential vulgarity. He had not made himself. It was even absurd to regret his transformation from an athlete: his greasy stoutness, his big black kiss-curl, his waxed moustache, his chin which was dividing and propagating itself like some primitive form of life. In England, nearly twenty years before, she had altered his figure as well as his character. He was one of the products of "The Eternal Moment."

A great tenderness overcame her—the sadness of an unskilful demiurge, who makes a world and beholds that it is bad. She desired to ask pardon of her creatures, even though they were too poorly formed to grant it. The longing to confess, which she had suppressed that morning beside the bed of Signora Cantù, broke out again with the violence of a physical desire. When the bishop had gone she renewed the conversation, though on different lines, saying: "Yes, it is beautiful weather. I have just been enjoying a walk up from the *Biscione*. I am stopping there!"

He saw that she was willing to talk, and replied pleasantly: "The *Biscione* must be a very nice hotel: many people speak well of it. The fresco is very beautiful." He was too shrewd to object to a little charity.

"What lots of new hotels there are!" She lowered her voice in order not to rouse the Prince, whose presence weighed on her curiously.

"Oh, madam! I should indeed think so. When I was a lad—Excuse me one moment."

An American girl, who was new to the country, came up with her hand full of coins, and asked him hopelessly "whatever they were worth." He explained, and gave her change: Miss Raby was not sure that he gave her right change.

"When I was a lad——" He was again interrupted, to speed two parting guests. One of them tipped him; he said, "Thank you." The other did not tip him; he said, "Thank you," all the same but not in the same way. Obviously he had as yet no recollections of Miss Raby.

"When I was a lad, Vorta was a poor little place."

"But a pleasant place?"

"Very pleasant, madam."

"Kouf!" said the Russian Prince, suddenly waking up and startling them both. He clapped on a felt hat, and departed at full speed for a constitutional. Miss Raby and Feo were left together.

It was then that she ceased to hesitate, and determined to remind him that they had met before. All day she had sought for a spark of life, and it might be summoned by pointing to that other fire which she discerned, far back in the travelled distance, high up in the mountains of youth. What he would do, if he also discerned it, she did not know; but she hoped that he would become alive, that he at all events would escape the general doom which she had prepared for the place and the people. And what she would do, during their joint contemplation, she did not even consider.

She would hardly have ventured if the sufferings of the day had not hardened her. After much pain, respectability becomes ludicrous. And she had only to overcome the difficulty of Feo's being a man, not the difficulty of his being a concierge. She had never observed that spiritual reticence towards social inferiors which is usual at the present day.

"This is my second visit," she said boldly. "I stayed at the *Biscione* twenty years ago."

He showed the first sign of emotion: *that* reference to the *Biscione* annoyed him.

"I was told I should find you up here," continued Miss Raby. "I remember you very well. You used to take us over the passes."

She watched his face intently. She did not expect it to relax into an expansive smile. "Ah!" he said, taking off his peaked cap, "I remember you perfectly, madam. What a pleasure, if I may say so, to meet you again!"

"I am pleased, too," said the lady, looking at him doubtfully.

"You and another lady, madam, was it not? Miss——"

"Mrs. Harbottle."

"To be sure; I carried your luggage. I often remember your kindness."

She looked up. He was standing near an open window, and the whole of fairyland stretched behind him. Her sanity forsook her, and she said gently: "Will you misunderstand me, if I say that I have never forgotten your kindness either?"

He replied: "The kindness was yours, madam; I only did my duty."

"Duty?" she cried; "what about duty?"

"You and Miss Harbottle were such generous ladies. I well remember how grateful I was: you always paid me above the tariff fare——"

Then she realized that he had forgotten everything; forgotten her, forgotten what had happened, even forgotten what he was like when he was young.

"Stop being polite," she said coldly. "You were not polite when I saw you last."

"I am very sorry," he exclaimed, suddenly alarmed.

"Turn round. Look at the mountains."

"Yes, yes." His fishy eyes blinked nervously. He fiddled with his watch chain which lay in a furrow of his waistcoat. He ran away to warn some poorly dressed children off the view-terrace. When he returned she still insisted.

"I must tell you," she said, in calm, business-like tones. "Look at that great mountain, round which the road goes south. Look half-way up, on its eastern side—where the flowers are. It was there that you once gave yourself away."

He gaped at her in horror. He remembered. He was inexpressibly shocked.

It was at that moment that Colonel Leyland returned.

She walked up to him, saying, "This is the man I spoke of yesterday."

"Good afternoon; what man?" said Colonel Leyland fussily. He saw that she was flushed, and concluded that some one had been rude to her. Since their relations were somewhat anomalous, he was all the more particular that she should be treated with respect.

"The man who fell in love with me when I was young."

"It is untrue!" cried the wretched Feo, seeing at once the trap that had been laid for him. "The lady imagined it. I swear, sir—I meant nothing. I was a lad. It was before I learnt behaviour. I had even forgotten it. She reminded me. She has disturbed me."

"Good Lord!" said Colonel Leyland. "Good Lord!"

"I shall lose my place, sir; and I have a wife and children. I shall be ruined."

"Sufficient!" cried Colonel Leyland. "Whatever Miss Raby's intentions may be, she does not intend to ruin you."

"You have misunderstood me, Feo," said Miss Raby gently.

"How unlucky we have been missing each other," said Colonel Leyland, in trembling tones that were meant to be nonchalant. "Shall we go a little walk before dinner? I hope that you are stopping."

She did not attend. She was watching Feo. His alarm had subsided; and he revealed a new emotion, even less agreeable to her. His shoulders straightened, he developed an irresistible smile, and, when he saw that she was looking and that Colonel Leyland was not, he winked at her.

It was a ghastly sight, perhaps the most hopelessly depressing of all the things she had seen at Vorta. But its effect on her was memorable. It evoked a complete vision of that same man as he had been twenty years before. She could see him to the smallest detail of his clothes or his hair, the flowers in his hand, the graze on his wrist, the heavy bundle that he had loosed from his back, so that he might speak as a freeman. She could hear his voice, neither insolent nor diffident, never threatening, never apologizing, urging her first in the studied phrases he had learnt from books, then, as his passion grew, becoming incoherent, crying that she must believe him, that she must love him in return, that she must fly with him to Italy, where they would live for ever, always happy, always young. She had cried out then, as a young lady should, and had thanked him not to insult her. And now, in her middle age, she cried out again, because the sudden shock and the contrast had worked a revelation. "Don't think I'm in love with you now!" she cried.

For she realized that only now was she not in love with him: that the incident upon the mountain had been one of the great moments of her life—perhaps the greatest, certainly the most enduring: that she had drawn unacknowledged power and inspiration from it, just as trees draw vigour from a subterranean spring. Never again could she think of it as a half-humorous episode in her development. There was more reality in it than in all the years of success and varied achievement which had followed, and which it had rendered possible. For all her correct behaviour and lady-like display, she had been in love with Feo, and she had never loved so greatly again. A presumptuous boy had taken her to the gates of heaven; and, though she would not enter with him, the eternal remembrance of the vision had made life seem endurable and good.

Colonel Leyland, by her side, babbled respectabilities, trying to pass the situation off as normal. He was saving her, for he liked her very much, and it pained him when she was foolish. But her last remark to Feo had frightened him; and he began to feel that he must save himself. They were no longer alone. The bureau lady and the young gentleman were listening breathlessly, and the porters were tittering at the discomfiture of their superior. A French lady had spread amongst the guests the agreeable news that an Englishman had surprised his wife making love to the concierge. On the terrace outside, a mother waved away her daughters. The bishop was preparing, very leisurely, for a walk.

But Miss Raby was oblivious. "How little I know!" she said. "I never knew till now that I had loved him and that it was a mere chance—a little catch, a kink—that I never told him so."

It was her habit to speak out; and there was no present passion to disturb or prevent her. She was still detached, looking back at a fire upon the mountains, marvelling at its increased radiance, but too far off to feel its heat. And by speaking out she believed, pathetically enough, that she was making herself intelligible. Her remark seemed inexpressibly coarse to Colonel Leyland.

"But these beautiful thoughts are a poor business, are they not?" she continued, addressing Feo, who was losing his gallant air, and becoming bewildered. "They're hardly enough to grow old on. I think I would give all my imagination, all my skill with words, if I could recapture one crude fact, if I could replace one single person whom I have broken."

"Quite so, madam," he responded, with downcast eyes.

"If only I could find some one here who would understand me, to whom I could confess, I think I should be happier. I have done so much harm in Vorta, dear Feo——"

Feo raised his eyes. Colonel Leyland struck his stick on the parquetry floor.

"—and at last I thought I would speak to you, in case you understood me. I remembered that you had once been very gracious to me—yes, gracious: there is no other word. But I have harmed you also: how could you understand?"

"Madam, I understand perfectly," said the concierge, who had recovered a little, and was determined to end the distressing scene, in which his reputation was endangered, and his vanity aroused only to be rebuffed. "It is you who are mistaken. You have done me no harm at all. You have benefited me."

"Precisely," said Colonel Leyland. "That is the conclusion of the whole matter. Miss Raby has been the making of Vorta."

"Exactly, sir. After the lady's book, foreigners come, hotels are built, we all grow richer. When I first came here, I was a common ignorant porter who carried luggage over the passes; I worked, I found opportunities, I was pleasing to the visitors—and now!" He checked himself suddenly. "Of course I am still but a poor man. My wife and children——"

"Children!" cried Miss Raby, suddenly seeing a path of salvation. "What children have you?"

"Three dear little boys," he replied, without enthusiasm.

"How old is the youngest?"

"Madam, five."

"Let me have that child," she said impressively, "and I will bring him up. He shall live among rich people. He shall see that they are not the vile creatures he supposes, always clamouring for respect and deference and trying to buy them with money. Rich people are good: they are capable of sympathy and love: they are fond of the truth; and when they are with each other they are clever. Your boy shall learn this, and he shall try to teach it to you. And when he grows up, if God is good to him he shall teach the rich: he shall teach them not to be stupid to the poor. I have tried myself, and people buy my books and say that they are good, and smile and lay them down. But I know this: so long as the stupidity exists, not only our charities and missions and schools, but the whole of our civilization, is vain."

It was painful for Colonel Leyland to listen to such phrases. He made one more effort to rescue Miss Raby. "Je vous prie de ne pas——" he began gruffly, and then stopped, for he remembered that the concierge must know French. But Feo was not attending, nor, of course, had he attended to the lady's prophecies. He was wondering if he could persuade his wife to give up the little boy, and, if he did, how much they dare ask from Miss Raby without repulsing her.

"That will be my pardon," she continued, "if out of the place where I have done so much evil I bring some good. I am tired of memories, though they have been very beautiful. Now, Feo, I want you to give me something else: a living boy. I shall always puzzle you; and I cannot help it. I have changed so much since we met, and I have changed you also. We are both new people. Remember that; for I want to ask you one question before we part, and I cannot see why you shouldn't answer it. Feo! I want you to attend."

"I beg your pardon, madam," said the concierge, rousing himself from his calculations. "Is there anything I can do for you?"

"Answer 'yes' or 'no'; that day when you said you were in love with me—was it true?"

It was doubtful whether he could have answered, whether he had now any opinion about that day at all. But he did not make the attempt. He saw again that he was menaced by an ugly, withered, elderly woman, who was trying to destroy his reputation and his domestic peace. He shrank towards Colonel Leyland, and faltered: "Madam, you must excuse me, but I had rather you did not see my wife; she is so sharp. You are most kind about my little boy; but, madam, no, she would never permit it."

"You have insulted a lady!" shouted the colonel, and made a chivalrous movement of attack. From the hall behind came exclamations of horror and expectancy. Some one ran for the manager.

Miss Raby interposed, saying, "He will never think me respectable." She looked at the dishevelled Feo, fat, perspiring, and unattractive, and smiled sadly at her own stupidity, not at his. It was useless to speak to him again; her talk had scared away his competence and his civility, and scarcely anything was left. He was hardly more human than a frightened rabbit. "Poor man," she murmured, "I have only vexed him. But I wish he would have given me the boy. And I wish he would have answered my question, if only out of pity. He does not know the sort of thing that keeps me alive." She was looking at Colonel Leyland, and so discovered that he too was discomposed. It was her peculiarity that she could only attend to the person she was speaking with, and forgot the personality of the listeners. "I have been vexing you as well: I am very silly."

"It is a little late to think about me," said Colonel Leyland grimly.

She remembered their conversation of yesterday, and understood him at once. But for him she had no careful explanation, no tender pity. Here was a man who was well born and well educated, who had all those things called advantages, who imagined himself full of insight and cultivation and knowledge of mankind. And he had proved himself to be at the exact spiritual level of the man who had no advantages, who was poor and had been made vulgar, whose early virtue had been destroyed by circumstance, whose manliness and simplicity had perished in serving the rich. If Colonel Leyland also believed that she was now in love with Feo, she would not exert herself to undeceive him. Nor indeed would she have found it possible.

From the darkening valley there rose up the first strong singing note of the campanile, and she turned from the men towards it with a motion of love. But that day was not to close without the frustration of every hope. The sound inspired Feo to make conversation and, as the mountains reverberated, he said: "Is it not unfortunate, sir? A gentleman went to see our fine new tower this morning and he believes that the land is slipping from underneath, and that it will fall. Of course it will not harm us up here."

His speech was successful. The stormy scene came to an abrupt and placid conclusion. Before they had realized it, she had taken up her *Baedeker* and left them, with no tragic gesture. In that moment of final failure, there had been vouchsafed to her a vision of herself, and she saw that she had lived worthily. She was conscious of a triumph over experience and earthly facts, a triumph magnificent, cold, hardly human, whose existence no one but herself would ever surmise. From the view-terrace she looked down on the perishing and perishable beauty of the valley, and, though she loved it no less, it seemed to be infinitely distant, like a valley in a star. At that moment, if kind voices had called her from the hotel, she would not have returned. "I suppose this is old age," she thought. "It's not so very dreadful."

No one did call her. Colonel Leyland would have liked to do so; for he knew she must be unhappy. But she had hurt him too much; she had exposed her thoughts and desires to a man of another class. Not only she, but he himself and all their equals, were degraded by it. She had discovered their nakedness to the alien.

People came in to dress for dinner and for the concert. From the hall there pressed out a stream of excited servants, filling the lounge as an operatic chorus fills the stage, and announcing the approach of the manager. It was impossible to pretend that nothing had happened. The scandal would be immense, and must be diminished as it best might.

Much as Colonel Leyland disliked touching people he took Feo by the arm, and then quickly raised his finger to his forehead.

"Exactly, sir," whispered the concierge. "Of course we understand——Oh, thank you, sir, thank you very much: thank you very much indeed!"